SO-AZU-973

APRIL HENRY

Torched

G. P. PUTNAM'S SONS

G. P. PUTNAM'S SONS
A division of Penguin Young Readers Group.
Published by The Penguin Group.
Penguin Group (USA) Inc., 375 Hudson Street, New York, NY 10014, U.S.A.
Penguin Group (Canada), 90 Eglinton Avenue East, Suite 700, Toronto,
Ontario M4P 2Y3, Canada (a division of Pearson Penguin Canada Inc.).
Penguin Books Ltd, 80 Strand, London WC2R 0RL, England.
Penguin Ireland, 25 St. Stephen's Green, Dublin 2, Ireland (a division of Penguin Books Ltd).
Penguin Group (Australia), 250 Camberwell Road, Camberwell, Victoria 3124, Australia
(a division of Pearson Australia Group Pty Ltd).
Penguin Books India Pvt Ltd, 11 Community Centre, Panchsheel Park,
New Delhi—110 017, India.
Penguin Group (NZ), 67 Apollo Drive, Rosedale, North Shore 0632, New Zealand
(a division of Pearson New Zealand Ltd).
Penguin Books (South Africa) (Pty) Ltd, 24 Sturdee Avenue, Rosebank,
Johannesburg 2196, South Africa.
Penguin Books Ltd, Registered Offices: 80 Strand, London WC2R 0RL, England.

Library of Congress Cataloging-in-Publication Data
Henry, April.
Torched / April Henry.   p. cm.
Summary: In order to save her parents from going to jail for possession of marijuana, sixteen-
year-old Ellie must help the FBI uncover the intentions of a radical environmental group by
going undercover.
[1. Ecoterrorism—Fiction. 2. Terrorism—Fiction. 3. Undercover operations—Fiction.]
I. Title.   PZ7.H39356To 2009   [Fic]—dc22   2008001145

ISBN 978-0-399-24645-6
10 9 8 7 6 5 4 3 2 1

For Kenzie:
Thank you for sharing your name—
and the fun!

Also by April Henry

Shock Point

PROLOGUE

Hugging the sloshing milk jug to her chest with her slick vinyl gloves, Sky hurried after Meadow and Coyote. The stench of gasoline and diesel made her sick to her stomach. She was shaking, and not just from the chill of the April night.

"Now!" Coyote whispered. The three of them dashed across the street toward the car dealership. They all ran a little awkwardly, thanks to the too-large thrift-store shoes they wore, the toes stuffed with newspaper so no one could trace them by their footprints. When a pebble clattered into the darkness ahead of them, Sky flinched, even though the security guard had just driven off and wouldn't be back for a long time.

Earlier in the week, Coyote and Sky had spent three nights in a parked car monitoring the security situation. It turned out to be pretty minimal. Every two hours the same guy wove his white and green private security car through the empty streets and then drove away. This part of town was dead quiet at night, a sea of car dealerships and long, windowless industrial buildings. Aside from the security guard's car, there was no real traffic.

Now Coyote nudged her. He grinned and jerked his chin at the banner over their heads. **HOT DEALS ON NEW HUMMERS!**

The three teens set down their jugs at the edge of the car

dealership lot and checked their watches. Sky's said 3:27. She had been awake for nearly twenty-four hours, but she had never felt less tired in her life.

Coyote held up one hand, fingers spread wide. He bunched them together and flicked them out three times. They had fifteen minutes.

They picked up their jugs and scattered to different parts of the lot. The dealership was a place of light and shadows. Along the edges that bordered the road, where a passing driver might stare longingly at a new SUV, it was brightly lit. But between the rows were deep gullies of black, and Sky ran down one of them now.

When she was in the middle of the row, she put down her jug and pulled a can of spray paint from the pocket of her hoodie. To her left, Meadow's giggle mingled with the hissing of the paint can. Sky shook her own can, then aimed the nozzle at the side of a black Hummer. She made a white wavy line along the side, wincing a little when it strayed up onto a window, feeling like a kindergartner trying not to color outside the lines.

On the hood, Sky painted I ♥ POLLUTION, then sprayed another wiggly line on the driver's side of the car. She pressed the button to light up her watch. 3:30. Three minutes gone. She worked faster now, running from car to car. On the front of one she wrote KILLER! On another she wrote FAT LAZY AMERICANS! Other Hummers received stars and hearts and more wavy lines. On the car at the end of the row, she wrote, THE MEDICS ARE HEALING THE EARTH, although she ran out of space and had to write the word *Earth* kind of small.

She checked her watch again. 3:41. Almost time to light the fuse.

Sky dropped the nearly empty can of spray paint. She had never littered before, but like Coyote said, you didn't want to get caught with a can of spray paint the same color as the one used at an action.

In the darkness, it took her several long seconds to find her jug of gasoline and diesel. Sky knelt down, the gravel poking her knees through her jeans, and felt for the homemade fuse held in place by a sponge. Crawling under one of the monstrous vehicles, she pushed the milk jug ahead of her until it sat squarely under the engine. After creeping out, she stood and shuffled backward, carefully unrolling the fuse until she was twenty feet away.

3:42. It was time.

But before Sky could move, her watch changed to 3:43.

She was late.

As she pulled the lighter from her pocket, she couldn't believe she was really doing this. Crouched down next to a huge black tire, she flicked the lighter's wheel. It didn't catch. She tried again. Nothing.

"Hurry!" someone hissed from behind her. She couldn't tell if it was Coyote or Meadow.

Desperate, she yanked off her glove and spun the lighter's wheel hard. The tiny serrations bit into her thumb.

Finally, a small flame appeared, flickered, threatening to go out. Hands shaking, Sky cupped the lighter, managing to keep the flame alive long enough to touch it to the end of the fuse. A tiny orange-blue light appeared. It began to race along the string. She stripped off the other glove and dropped it as she scrambled to her feet.

She turned and ran. At one point she tripped over her too-big shoes and scraped one knee, but in less than a second she was back on her feet. Her ears strained for the first sound. When it came, it was so loud that it was more of a physical sensation than noise.

Whoomp! Thick air pushed past her, slapping her left ear. And then another explosion, even louder, this time on her right. Sky ran harder, her breath coming in gulps. She had to get out of the lot before the whole thing was a fireball.

Behind her she heard smaller explosions as gas tanks added their own fuel to the fire. She burst across the street to where Coyote and Meadow gestured frantically. Coyote had just pulled her behind the shelter of a Dumpster when the third explosion came.

She peered around the corner at the dealership.

My God, she thought, *we did that. Three kids did that!*

Even across the street, it was like standing in front of an open oven. The three fires had grown into one, its long orange flames licking the sky. Above it, a pillar of thick, black smoke floated up to blot out the stars. The whole thing was strangely beautiful.

All Sky's fear was now gone. She soaked in the sensations, the heat tightening her skin, the hungry growl of the fire, the bright flames, the dusty taste of ashes and the mingled smells of gasoline, plastic, leather and rubber, all of it burning.

"Run, Sky! Run!" Meadow shouted. She jerked Sky's arm,

breaking the spell. They bolted away from the dealership. The long blank buildings ahead of them glowed as if lit by a summer sunset. They cut through parking lots, keeping close to the edges of buildings, and then through another dealership, zigging and zagging. Behind them, Sky heard sirens.

They threw themselves into the car. Meadow grabbed the shotgun seat. Coyote shoved the key in the ignition, and they took off.

"Woo-hoo!" he shouted. "We did it!" In his excitement, his voice broke, but he didn't seem to notice, or care. It was the kind of thing that had made Sky fall in love with Coyote.

Meadow turned in the seat and shot Sky a look from underneath her straight black bangs, one that Coyote couldn't see.

"What took you so long, anyway, Sky? I was worried you were going to be toast. Literally." As she spoke, Meadow pulled off her dark sweatshirt. In addition to their shoes, the top layer of their clothes had come from thrift stores and would now go into a grocery store's Dumpster.

"I couldn't get the lighter to light," Sky said. "The glove made my thumb too smooth. Finally I just took it off."

"You took off your glove?" Meadow pulled her T-shirt down into place. "So where's your lighter?"

"I left it there." As soon as Sky said it, she realized this was the wrong answer.

Meadow's mouth fell open. Coyote turned to stare, whipping his head back when a police car came barreling toward them.

The cop car passed without slowing down. "I had to take it off," Sky said. "I couldn't get the lighter to work."

"You better hope it got burned up," Meadow said, looking half scared and half triumphant at Sky's mistake. "What if the cops pull your fingerprints off it?"

Sky tried to look worried, but she knew it wouldn't matter.

Because it was the cops—really, the FBI—who had asked her to be part of this in the first place.

CHAPTER ONE

I stood in the hallway and listened at the closed living room door. It was my turn to cook dinner, but I didn't know how many people to make it for. There were too many voices to count.

The doorbell had rung an hour earlier while I was upstairs doing my English lit homework. Now it sounded like Laurel and Matt were having some kind of meeting. I wondered what they were involved in this week. Saving the whales, expanding gay rights, lobbying for universal health care? Every week there was another cause.

It wasn't that I disagreed with their choices. I mean, it was a lot better than if they were picketing abortion clinics. But it never really seemed like any of Laurel and Matt's signs and petitions made much of a difference.

Laurel and Matt were my parents, but they didn't like to be called Mom and Dad. They believed the terms "Mom" and "Dad" were "constructs of a hierarchical society." Or something like that. The way they said the words, you could tell they had quote marks around them.

There were times when I secretly wished they were like normal parents. That they both wore suits to their office jobs and on Friday nights we went to the Olive Garden for dinner.

But instead of a job in an office, Laurel volunteered for various causes, grew most of our own food in the backyard and put in stints at the food co-op. Matt was a freelance computer programmer who dressed in flannel shirts and jeans and worked from home. Both of them wore Birkenstocks, and Laurel never wore a bra. We never had much money, but according to them, we didn't need much.

Years ago, my parents had lived in a commune, and they still believed in sharing whatever they had. Our dinners usually felt like a casual church potluck or a communal table at a vegetarian restaurant. There might be an antiwar activist at our table one day, or some people Laurel had met at the food co-op the next.

I slid open the pocket door to the living room. "Excuse me for interrupting. How many should I make dinner for?"

The conversation stopped in midstream. Eight heads swiveled in my direction. This wasn't the normal group of ex-hippies my parents usually hung out with. A couple of them seemed about my age, sixteen, and the rest didn't look that much older. I didn't recognize any of them from Wilson High. Which was good. It would have been way too embarrassing.

The room reeked of pot. God, sometimes I couldn't believe my parents. They grew their own weed in the basement and would light up with just about anyone—people they barely knew, old baby boomers like them and now kids *my* age. I kept telling them that someday they were going to get caught, but they said they had been smoking pot for thirty years and they weren't about to stop now. Sometimes I felt more like I was the parent and they were the kids.

The only person from Wilson that I let come over was my best friend, Marijean. Kids at school thought my parents were weird enough as it was. It would be infinitely worse if they thought they could score off them.

"This is our daughter, Ellie," Laurel said into the sudden silence. She waved her hand at the people in the room. "These folks are working on, um, an environmental campaign."

"So is everybody staying for dinner?" I asked. "I'm making pasta, so it can get stretched pretty easy."

Before anyone answered, they all looked at this guy with black hair combed straight back. Even from fifteen feet away, I could see that his eyes were a piercing blue. He was probably the oldest of the group, but still thirty years younger than my parents. He nodded and then Laurel said, "Of course everyone is staying! Thank you, honey."

But I barely heard Laurel, because my eyes were caught by a guy with tight golden ringlets that just brushed his shoulders. *God, he was gorgeous!* He was tall and slim, but with wiry muscles. His tanned skin was set off by his white T-shirt. On the front, it said WHAT GOES AROUND COMES AROUND with a picture of a green recycling symbol. He looked a year or two older than me.

His eyes met mine, and then he smiled. It felt like a bolt of lightning flickered between us. My cheeks flushed, and I quickly looked away.

Telling myself to calm down, I counted heads. My parents and I made three. The gorgeous guy was four, the older guy was five, a girl with red dreads was six, a tiny girl with blond pigtails was seven (she grinned at me, and I returned it), a creepy-looking guy with eyes that seemed too big for his head was eight and a girl with black bangs cut straight across made nine. But it was the cute guy with the ringlets I couldn't stop thinking about.

Remembering that old saying—the way to a man's heart is through his stomach—I hurried into the kitchen. I diced some onions and started sautéing them, then got out our battered old *Joy of Cooking*. From the fridge, I pulled milk, butter, eggs and three pints of strawberries. I had planned on making pasta and a salad, but strawberry shortcake wouldn't take that long.

An hour later, dinner was served. There wasn't room enough for everyone around the table, so I got a folding chair from the closet and set my plate on my knees. My heart started pounding when I saw the cute guy pick up another chair and carry it in my direction.

He opened it up and set it down next to me. "So you're Laurel and Matt's daughter, huh? My name's Coyote." His eyes were a light yellow-green, like a cat's. I realized that I was staring and looked back down at my plate.

"Coyote?" *Thank God my parents didn't name me anything weird, like so many of their friends did with their kids.* "My name's Ellie."

"Coyote's kind of my stage name," he said.

"Are you guys actors?"

"All the world's a stage," Coyote said, and laughed. I laughed, too, although I didn't really get the joke. I snuck a quick look at him again. One of his front teeth had been broken and mended, leaving a line of bright white in the center. Every time Coyote spoke, that flash of white drew my eye.

The girl with red dreadlocks opened up another folding chair and sat down next to Coyote, so close their thighs touched. She wore one of those hand-knit imported sweaters that you can buy at Portland's outdoor Saturday Market from some Peruvian-looking guy who also sells panpipes. Was she trying to tell me something? Probably. Well, it had been nice while it lasted.

"This is Liberty," Coyote said. "Liberty, this is Ellie." Liberty tilted her head a teeny bit, looking bored, like a queen forced to meet the commoners. Coyote introduced me to the rest of them: Meadow was the girl with the black bangs. The friendly girl with the blond pigtails was Blue. The guy with the too-big eyes was Hawk. And the older guy that everyone had looked to when Laurel asked about dinner was Cedar. I noticed how everyone catered to him—making a place for him at the center of the table, handing him the first plate of food.

"Even if you look at it from a Machiavellian standpoint, it makes sense," Matt said, clearly continuing the conversation they'd been having in the living room. "We're killing this world, but we depend on it to survive. If we ruin it, where will we live?" Some tomato sauce sprayed out of his mouth as he talked. I winced, but no one else seemed to notice.

"Exactly," Coyote said, getting up to dish up more spaghetti from one of our chipped red Mexican serving dishes. "Most adults don't even hear what we're saying. All they think about is what they're going to buy next. Or they say we're not being practical, that they only have time to worry about paying the mortgage and getting their kids off to college."

Liberty shook her head. "Except at the rate we're going,

their kids won't be able to survive in this messed-up world, let alone go to college." She was so intense that her red dreads looked like they could give off sparks.

Coyote sat back down. "This food is really good, Ellie," he said.

Maybe the old saying *was* right. And he hadn't even tasted the strawberry shortcake yet.

"Thanks." I didn't trust myself to look at his face for very long. What if I forgot to blink? I focused on his hands instead. Coyote had long, tanned, strong-looking fingers.

"Who wants dessert?" Laurel asked, beginning to dish it up. "If you think Ellie's pasta is good, wait until you taste her strawberry shortcake." She passed the first plate to Blue, who smacked her lips. She was so tiny she reminded me of a sprite or a fairy.

"No whipped cream for me," Liberty righteously declared. "I'm a vegan."

I decided to keep it to myself that the shortcake had an egg yolk in it for extra richness and passed her the plate Laurel handed me.

After dinner was over, everyone carried their dishes into the kitchen. While the rest straggled back to the living room, Coyote said, "Need any help with washing up?"

Is he just being polite—or is it something more? "Sure. Do you want to wash or dry?" With shaking hands, I turned on the faucet and started filling the sink with hot water.

"Dry." He started picking up plates that still had leftover food on them. I was proud to see there weren't many.

"So you guys put on plays about the environment or some-thing?" I asked as Coyote scraped the plates into the compost bin. "Back in middle school, this band came to assembly and sang about how we needed to save water and energy." I didn't mention that they were really hokey. One of them wore a suit of armor made from tin cans.

He smiled. "That was more of a joke."

"Oh." Suddenly I felt like *I* was back in middle school. "Then what do you guys do?"

Coyote's expression turned totally serious. "You can't tell, okay?"

I set down the plate I held. "Tell about what?"

Even though we were alone in the kitchen, Coyote leaned closer. He lowered his voice to a whisper and put his lips close to my ear. His breath stirred the hairs on my neck, making me shiver.

"We're Mother Earth Defenders."

I pulled back. I had read about them in the paper, some-times seen them on the news. "You mean those people who sit in trees so the loggers won't cut them down?"

"That—and a few other things. But we try to keep a low profile when we're not doing an action. There are a lot of peo-ple who don't like what we're doing and would stop us if they could."

Things were starting to fall into place. "A lot of my parents' friends gave their kids weird names. But I kind of figured there were too many of you for that to be true."

He shrugged. "It's safer if we don't use our real names."

"Coyote's cool, but if it *was* your real name, you'd probably get a lot of grief. At my high school everyone is into wearing the same clothes, having the same hairstyle, doing the same things. They want you to fit into one of their predetermined little groups, you know, the smart kids, or the jocks, or the drama geeks, or the people whose parents have a lot of money. They don't like people who are different."

"So where do you fit in?" Coyote asked.

"Me? I'm kind of in a group of one. Maybe two," I added, thinking of Marijean. Because of a car accident, her dad used a wheelchair. Her mom left a long time ago. She knew what it was like to have parents you're sort of embarrassed by at the school open house.

He nodded, looking thoughtful. I didn't tell him that growing up with my parents guaranteed you had to march to a different drummer. I had pretty much spent my whole life feeling like I didn't fit in anyplace.

"So where do you go to school?" I asked. He was still standing right next to me. I didn't know if it was my imagination, but I thought I could feel the heat from his body.

"Oh, I've already got my GED and live on my own. I work at the bike shop in Multnomah."

Coyote suddenly seemed a lot older. I couldn't imagine already being done with school. "Really? How old are you? I mean, if you don't mind my asking."

"I'll be eighteen in August. Last year I talked my parents into letting me be an emancipated minor and take my GED."

"Wow," I said. "That must be cool." Suddenly, I wondered if Matt and Laurel would let me do that. Or if I wanted to. My parents always said you needed to go to college to expand your mind.

Coyote gave me a half smile. "It has its moments. But I like working in Multnomah. It's a pretty cool place."

Multnomah Village was a Portland neighborhood about ten blocks from our house. In the center was a little cluster of stores and restaurants where you could buy gelato or funky shoes, or pick up something at the bakery or the bookstore.

Or you could get your bike fixed. I suddenly wished I had a bike.

Coyote gave me a smile. "Stop by next time you're in the area, okay? I can take a break and buy you a cup of tea."

I nodded. My veins felt like they were buzzing. Like they were filled with tiny bubbles instead of blood.

CHAPTER TWO

The Boer War. Had anything ever been so aptly named?

While Ms. Tamson, my history teacher, droned on about Sir Theophilus Shepstone annexing the Transvaal Republic in 1877, I stared out the window and thought about Coyote. Normally, I paid attention at school, but right now all I could concentrate on was finding a way to work the name Sir Theophilus Shepstone into conversation the next time I saw Coyote. I imagined the bright line of his mended tooth flashing when he laughed.

I yawned again, barely managing to get my hand up to my mouth in time. I had been up all night, wondering and worrying. Did Coyote think I was cute? Or was he just being friendly? Did offering to buy me a cup of tea count as a date? I had been on a grand total of two dates in my life, and neither one of the guys had looked anything like Coyote. But if it wasn't a date, what was it? And what about Liberty? Was she his girlfriend or not?

Finally, the bell rang. I pushed my way through the halls and out the front door. Freedom!

On the sidewalk, I met Marijean. Marijean made her own jewelry, and today she wore a necklace she had made out of beads, tiny gears from an old bike and walnut shells she had carved into twisting shapes. A lot of it was stuff you didn't realize could be pretty or useful until she strung it on a colorful piece of telephone wire.

I did basically the same thing, only with clothes. Laurel and Matt bought most of our clothes at Value Village, and a few years ago, I realized that my clothes didn't have to be limited to how they looked when I found them on the rack. If I didn't fit in, I wanted it to be because I was *me*, not because I was poor. So now I ripped out seams from old clothes and used the pieces of fabric to create something completely different, like a sweater put together from three different sweaters. Or I covered stains or holes with appliqués and embroidery so that the worst part of a garment became the best.

As we started walking away from the school, Marijean took a pack of cigarettes out of her purse and lit one.

"I wish you wouldn't do that." I moved to the other side of the sidewalk so that the wind blew the smoke away from my face.

"I don't know why you don't," Marijean said. "Your parents sure wouldn't give you any crap for it."

"Actually, Matt and Laurel would mind. They think pot's natural, but they hate cigarettes. The other day they had a bunch of new friends over and our house reeked. And half of them were *our* age. You can imagine how weird that was."

"Our age?" Marijean grinned, then pursed her lips and blew a smoke ring. "Were there any cute guys?"

"Maybe." I smiled and looked away.

"Maybe?" She nudged me. "Spill!"

"There was this one guy who calls himself Coyote. He's got these green eyes like a cat's and really tight curls down to his shoulders."

"Coyote?" Marijean raised one eyebrow, making the little silver hoop she wears there wiggle. "What kind of a name is that? Are his parents old hippies, too?"

"Kind of." I shrugged, remembering how he had asked me not to tell about the MEDics. It was kind of weird keeping something from Marijean, but I told myself it wasn't a big deal.

"Where does he go to school?"

"He doesn't. He's seventeen, but he's an emancipated minor and he's got his GED."

"That's sweet!"

"He works at the bike shop in Multnomah. But there was this other girl at our house with red dreads hanging around him. She seemed pissed off that he was talking to me."

Marijean blew another ring of smoke. "I hate dreads on white people."

"Me too. Anyway, Coyote told me I should stop by the bike shop and he'd take me out for tea."

"No way!" Marijean cuffed my shoulder. "Ooh, it sounds like he *does* like you. So are you going to do it?"

"Of course." Just thinking about Coyote made me feel like dancing. Instead, I skipped a few steps along the sidewalk. We turned into the little strip of shops in Hillsdale. "What do you think I should wear?"

"How about that black sweater with the patterned silk sleeves?" I had taken a short-sleeved sweater and sewn a three-inch-wide stripe of emerald-green fabric at the bottom of each sleeve. Under that I had added another stripe of wild abstract fabric patterned with golds and oranges. It was beautiful. There was only one problem. "That actually sold on Etsy.com." We both sold—or at least tried to sell—things on Etsy.com, along with a million other people who made stuff.

"Too bad. Maybe you can find something here." Marijean pushed open the door to Zombie, a vintage store that was usually too expensive for us. Normally we scavenged things from garage sales or went to the Bins—officially the Goodwill Outlet Store, but nobody called it that—where you could buy stuff by the pound. Still, it was always fun to look.

I started going through the sale rack. The edge of an ornately patterned sweater caught my eye. But when I pulled it from the rack, the wool felt too thick. The whole thing was too small to fit anyone but a little kid.

"Somebody forgot to check the temperature on the wash cycle." I held the shrunken sweater out to Marijean, who teetered up to me on a giant pair of go-go boots. Even with six-inch platforms she was just barely eye-to-eye with me.

"The pattern is cool, though." She fingered it, then nearly lost her balance and grabbed onto me. "You could run it through the washer again, put it in the dryer on high and make it into felt for appliqués."

"Yeah," I said slowly, "I've got a black sweater I could put them on. It's kind of low-cut, though."

"And that's a problem?" Marijean asked.

I thought of Coyote again and smiled. "No, I guess it really isn't."

CHAPTER THREE

A bell tinkled over my head as I pushed open the door to the Multnomah Bicycle Shop. I didn't want to look too eager, so after consulting with Marijean, I had decided to wait until late Saturday afternoon before I stopped by.

I had lasted until 11:17 A.M.

At first I didn't see him, just an older guy sitting at a battered desk and looking through a parts catalog. Part of me was almost relieved. Now I wouldn't have to find out how Coyote felt about me. But then I spotted him in the back of the room. He was working on a bike that had been flipped upside down on top of a long, scarred table. His hands were covered with grease, his face intent as his long fingers followed a kinked chain. Above him, a couple dozen bikes hung from the high ceiling.

When he saw me, his face smoothed out into a smile. "Hey, George, is it okay if I take a break?" he asked.

The other man grinned. "Sure, Ethan."

Ethan? It was strange to think that Coyote had another name. A real name. It didn't seem to fit him as well as Coyote did.

"A loooong break?" Coyote drew out the word. I looked down at the toes of my clogs.

George only laughed. While Coyote hung up his apron and washed his hands in the sink, I wondered how many girls had stood here before me. He dried his hands, grabbed a mug from a shelf over the sink, lifted up the hinged counter and walked out to join me.

"That's a cool sweater," he said.

I wore the low-cut sweater Marijean had suggested, only now it had cutout paisley shapes from the shrunken sweater I had bought at Zombie. I couldn't tell if Coyote was looking at the sweater or the V-neck. I was just glad that he was looking. "Thanks. I made it. I like to take things I find and make them useful again."

"I like it," he said as we walked down the street. "It's different."

"Speaking of different, it was kind of weird to hear him call you Ethan. I guess you seem more like a Coyote. At least to me. Once I saw a real coyote." As the words kept tumbling out of my mouth, I realized how stupid I sounded. I ordered myself to stop talking, but instead I kept babbling. "It was early in the morning and I was running by Gabriel Park. It's strange to think they can live in the middle of a city."

Coyote made a face. "Too bad we've forced so many animals to make that choice, adapt to us or die." His words came easily. He probably had had lots of different girlfriends. Including the girl with the red dreads.

We waited for a TriMet bus to pass, then crossed the street. "I took my MEDic name in honor of a coyote I saw a couple of years ago, in the Portland airport parking lot," Coyote continued. "We had just come back from Hawaii, and it was, like, three in the morning. At first, I thought it was a dog that had been hurt, you know, because of the way it ran." Coyote demonstrated, loping ahead a few steps. He waited for me to catch up. "Then I realized it was a coyote. I stuck my head out the window and howled at it." He grinned at the memory. "My dad didn't much like that."

"What's your dad like?"

Coyote pressed his lips together before answering. "A consumer. He's a stockbroker. We don't have a lot in common. He doesn't have that much in common with my mom, either."

"Do your parents mind that you aren't going to school and you're not living at home?"

"Are you kidding?" Coyote gave me a twist of a smile. "It kills my dad. Absolutely kills him."

He held open the door to Village Coffee. It was only a block from a Starbucks, but the two places couldn't have been less alike. Village Coffee was small and cluttered, but I liked going there because there was always a new piece of art on the walls, a new magnetic poem on the cash register or old esoteric magazines scattered on the tables. It was one of a kind.

"Tall skinny latte," I told the barista, who had sideburns to rival Elvis's. "Two shots."

Coyote reached past me with a ten-dollar bill. "I'm paying for it."

"Oh, no. That's okay. I can buy my own coffee." I waved my own five-dollar bill at the guy.

Coyote handed over his mug and the money to the barista. "Lemon ginger tea, please." He turned to me. "You can buy next time."

Next time. I had to fight back a grin. Maybe this *was* a date.

We sat down at a table in the corner. Feeling emboldened by "next time," I decided to tease him a little. "Isn't this Village *Coffee*?" I said as he used a spoon to press the tea bag against the side of his mug. "Why did you get tea?"

"It's so hard to know if the coffee's fair-trade, you know, or how many pesticides they sprayed it with," he said.

I clutched my latte protectively. "What about your tea? How do you know what they spray on it or who picks it and how much they get paid?"

"Touché!" said Coyote, lifting his mug to click with my paper cup. "I probably sound like I'm full of crap. But I am trying to make a difference in what I choose to support, even if sometimes it doesn't feel like it adds up to much. I want to leave the world in better condition than how I found it. That's what I like about your parents. They get it."

"Where do you . . ." I hesitated, not wanting to mention the word *MEDics* in public, even if no one was sitting next to us. "Where do you guys know my parents from?"

"Hawk met them at the food co-op. They're pretty cool for—" He stopped.

I finished his sentence. "For old people. They *are* old. They're not my biological parents, anyway. They adopted me when I was a baby."

Coyote's green eyes widened. "Do you know who your real parents are?"

"Just that they were in high school. I guess they knew they couldn't hack both school and a baby. So Laurel and Matt adopted me."

"They don't mind if you call them by their first names? My dad would kill me."

"They think it sounds too subservient if I call them Mom and Dad."

Coyote looked impressed. I didn't tell him that I sometimes wished for parents who were a little more normal. It was okay when my parents were around their own friends or even Marijean. But every time we were out doing something and ran into someone from school, I couldn't help but feel self-conscious. Matt with his long gray hair and beard and Laurel with her belief that bras were "unnatural."

I took a sip of my coffee. "They never hid it from me that I was adopted," I said. "I guess they figured it wouldn't take me too long to figure out that they were too old to be my real parents. Sometimes I wish I had someone I looked like or that I took after. You know, like I had the same color hair as my grandmother, or an aunt who played the piano like me."

Coyote's long fingers played with his tea bag. "There's a downside to relatives, though. Take my grandfather. He's old school—hunting, fishing, having everything stuffed and mounted. I remember being at his house one time when I was a little kid. I tried to pet this animal by the fireplace, and then I got all freaked out when I realized it was hard and dead.

Then when I was fourteen and hunting season came around, he insisted that I had to get my first buck. I told him no way, but he wouldn't listen."

"What happened?" I asked.

"We got all dressed up in blaze orange and went out in the woods. We walked around forever until we saw a buck." His mouth pulled down at the corners. "It was beautiful. Majestic. I still remember how it turned and looked at us. I fired twenty feet over its head, but it still fell over dead."

"How did that happen?"

"Because my grandpa had shot it at the same time." Coyote raised his face to mine, his green eyes glittering. "Then he slapped me on the back and congratulated me on my kill."

CHAPTER FOUR

For the next few days, I was too distracted by my time with Coyote to pay attention to teachers or homework. When I talked to Marijean, my only topic was Coyote. Like a true friend, she listened patiently, even when I repeated myself. I just couldn't stop thinking about him. We had traded cell numbers, but I had been too nervous to call him.

When I came home from school on Thursday, the pocket door to the living room was closed again. I set my backpack down on the hall table and sniffed the air. Pot. And with people over, too—I heard the low murmur of voices.

"We're in here, Ellie," Laurel called out.

I slid open the door. The first person I saw was Coyote, who looked up and smiled at me. I grinned back, then tried to tamp it down. All the MEDics I had met before—Coyote, Meadow, Blue, Liberty, Hawk and Cedar—were crowded into the living room, along with some other people I didn't recognize. The sweet smell of weed hung heavy in the air, but there were no joints in evidence—just cups of ginger tea.

"Want to join us?" Laurel asked.

Hawk, the skinny guy with the pop eyes, said, "I really don't know about . . ."

Matt chuckled. "Ellie's been going to demonstrations since she was a three-month-old in a baby sling."

I saw Liberty nudge Meadow, the girl with the black Cleopatra bangs. Both of them rolled their eyes and giggled. Then Meadow saw that I had noticed and looked away.

Didn't Matt have a clue about what was embarrassing? I didn't want these people to think of me like I was still a baby.

Cedar cleared his throat. Immediately, everyone looked to him. "Of course she can stay," he said. No one said anything after that, although Hawk pressed his thin lips together so tight they disappeared.

Even though I longed to sit by Coyote, I didn't want to be too obvious. So I sat on the floor between Cedar and Blue, the girl with the stubby blond pigtails.

Matt laced his fingers comfortably over his belly. "As I was saying, we were pretty active in the movement 'back in the day,' as you kids like to say."

I winced at Matt's lame attempt at slang. But the others looked interested.

"What did you do?" a young guy with a bowl haircut and rings on his thumbs asked.

"We did a lot, Jack Rabbit." Matt loosened his hands so that he could tick off examples on his fingers. "Teach-ins, prayer vigils, street theater, blockades. Organizing the unions, the military and the churches. Civil disobedience. We took over the college president's office and occupied it for thirty-three days."

I knew most of this. Once every six months or so, my parents would drink a couple of bottles of wine and get all misty-eyed about the glory days, thirty years ago. Last year, in social studies, we learned about hippies, sit-ins, the Vietnam

War, "sticking it to the man." For everyone else, it was ancient history.

Coyote said, "Two months ago we chained ourselves to the fence outside a timber company's corporate headquarters to protest water pollution."

"What was the outcome?" Laurel asked.

Meadow straightened up, her black bangs swinging. "I put out a communiqué. We got on channels six, eight and twelve." Her voice was full of pride.

Laurel gave her a polite smile. "The problem is that it's so easy to be marginalized. You end up being the human-interest story, the out-there protesters, something to run at the end of the local news. What you need to do is raise people's consciousness until they themselves are willing to act."

Meadow's face turned red. She nibbled on a fingernail. Now I didn't know who to be more embarrassed by, back-in-the-day Matt or lecturing Laurel.

But Hawk nodded in agreement. "Exactly. It takes more than being on TV. If people refuse to wake up, then we have to force them to by any means necessary. It's a matter of life and death—not just the death of individual species, but the death of the entire planet. And desperate times call for desperate measures."

Looking stern, Cedar said to my parents, "Forgive my friend Hawk here. He can be a little hot-blooded. It *is* vital that people start paying attention. But we need to remember our tenets: We do not harm people, animals or the environment in defense of the Earth."

"How did you get people to start paying attention back then, Matt?" Coyote asked. I was glad that he had said something, because it gave me an excuse to look at him. God, he was gorgeous. I imagined what it would be like if he really was my boyfriend. I'd buy a bike, and after school and on weekends we'd ride along the Eastside Esplanade, eat picnics in Forest Park, roam through Powell's bookstore. Village Coffee would be "our" place, where the barista knew what both of us liked to drink without even asking, where everyone knew which table was ours. Maybe Coyote would even wait for me outside school sometimes. I imagined all the stupid cheerleader girls' mouths falling open when they first caught sight of him.

While I daydreamed, Matt kept going. "What we cared about was more than just Vietnam. It was civil rights, women's rights, class warfare—we wanted to tear everything down and start on a level playing field." He made a sweeping gesture with his arms. "What turned things around for Vietnam was when people could turn on their TVs and see our soldiers dying in the jungle. That helped people reach a—what do they call it?—a tipping point. What we need for the environment is another tipping point. If we're lucky, people will naturally realize how important it is. If we're not, it will take a total disaster."

A guy with a bushy brown beard said, "Like, okay, we gotta do something now? Before something bad happens? Not just talk about doing something?" Even though he was a heavyset guy in his twenties, with what looked like bird bones in his pierced ears, his sentences all rose at the end, as if he were a teenage girl at Washington Square Mall.

"But we *have* taken action, Grizz," a woman with long blond hair said. With her buckteeth and pale skin, she reminded me of a rabbit.

"Action? Like what, Seed?" Matt leaned forward, enthralled.

Some of the other MED members exchanged glances, like they didn't want my parents and me to know. Hawk pressed his lips together again.

Seed lowered her voice, but her tone was proud. "We were the ones who liberated the four-legged captives from the Hillhurst Ranch."

Four-legged captives? I thought. *Wait—does she mean animals? Give me a break!*

Matt wrinkled his forehead. "You mean those minks?"

I had heard about that. The year before, a thousand minks had been released from a mink farm halfway between Portland and the coast. The newspaper had said many of them had died within a few days—through roadkill, starvation or by drowning in a backyard swimming pool.

Liberty nodded, setting her red dreads swinging. "The prisoners of the war on nature."

"But didn't a lot of them die anyway?" Laurel asked.

Liberty narrowed her eyes. "Maybe a few. But at least we gave them a shot at life. They had the chance to use their legs in freedom and to die on their own terms. When we were leaving, I could see one mink already beginning to burrow under a log, gathering twigs and grass to build a nest."

It was all I could do not to roll my eyes. Probably the poor mink had just been trying to hide from its rescuers. Killing minks for fur was stupid, but dumping farm-raised minks in the forest didn't necessarily sound like a better alternative.

Jack Rabbit stretched and yawned, then got to his feet. "Well, folks, I've got to go. Big test tomorrow."

After that, the group broke up. I loitered near the door, hoping to talk to Coyote. He lingered a few minutes, speaking to first Liberty and then Meadow. Both conversations were too low for me to follow. Telling myself I didn't care, I turned away and started gathering up cups. Then he walked over to me, and my heart did a flip.

He gave me an easy grin. "So how's your week been so far?"

"Good, good." I was nodding my head like an idiot and tried to stop. "How about yours?"

"Pretty tolerable. Of course, it would be better if I took more breaks. Will you be in Multnomah again this Saturday?"

I tried to look nonchalant. "Maybe. I could stop by if you want."

"Of course!" His fingers circled my wrist and gave it a squeeze before he slipped on his backpack. Before I could say anything else, he was out the door. The rest of the MEDics soon followed him. My skin tingled where he had touched me.

"Those kids are kind of cute when they get all excited," Laurel said as we picked up the mugs that held dregs of tea. "But when we were in college, what we were fighting for was life and death. We knew plenty of guys who went off to Vietnam and never came back."

"At least they're trying," Matt said. "That's a lot more than most kids these days. They remind me so much of us when we were young."

"So I saw that Coyote talking to you," Laurel said. "Do you like him?"

"I don't really know him that well." I bent down to pick up some more dishes, letting my hair fall forward to hide my face.

"Laurel and I knew the minute we saw each other," Matt said. "She had on her 'Anything War Can Do, Peace Can Do Better' T-shirt, and I had 'An Eye for an Eye Makes the Whole World Blind.' We even got arrested the same day. Remember, Laurel?" They shared a smile.

I carried the cups into the kitchen. Behind me, Matt was saying something more about the Vietnam protests, but the words were lost as I clattered the dishes in the sink. I heard one of them switch on the TV.

While my parents were occupied, I called Marijean. "You are not going to believe this, but Coyote just asked me to have coffee with him again! Well, tea, I guess. He drinks tea. I'm the one who drinks coffee."

"You're babbling." Marijean laughed.

"Do you think I should wear perfume?"

"I don't know. What if he kisses you? You don't want him to taste it if you've got perfume on your neck."

"I think you're talking about a little more than kissing," I said.

"I'm talking *enthusiastic* kissing," she said. "I'm an ex–Girl Scout. Isn't their motto 'Be prepared'? So if you wear perfume, just put it on your wrists."

After discussing every possible detail with Marijean, I finally flipped my cell phone closed. We had talked long enough that the plastic was warm. I still had homework to do, so I got a hunk of cheddar from the fridge and some Ak-Mak crackers. I alternated eating a bite of cracker and then a bite of cheese, trying to get my mind off Coyote and onto my math problems.

Soon I had two crackers left and no cheese, so I got up to get more. As I turned from the fridge, a glint of light in the front yard caught my eye.

A man, all dressed in black, was approaching the house.

The glint was a reflection from the silver badge he wore on his chest.

"Laurel! Matt!" I cried out. "Cops!"

From the living room came shouts and the sounds of wood splintering. A man burst in from the utility room between the kitchen and the garage. In his black-gloved hand, he held a gun. POLICE was spelled out in yellow letters on his black baseball cap. "Don't move!" he barked.

On the other side of the house, I heard shouts, orders, questions. Laurel cried out. It sounded like someone had hurt her. I tried to run to her, but the policeman grabbed my arm.

"I said don't move!"

"What's going on?" My voice shook.

He didn't answer.

A minute later, more cops marched my parents into the kitchen. Their wrists were handcuffed behind their backs.

"You're under arrest," one of the cops told them.

"For what?" Matt said defiantly, but he looked scared. He was breathing in big gulps, like a swimmer who had just escaped a rough sea. His face was red and blotchy, shiny with sweat.

"Drug dealing. We can talk about it down at the station."

"What about our daughter?" Laurel asked.

The cop holding my arm said, "Don't worry, we'll take care of her."

I could not believe this was happening.

As I watched Matt and Laurel being led outside, I couldn't breathe. When I went to the kitchen window, no one stopped me. After a cop came back in to grab a pair of shoes for Matt, they were taken to separate squad cars. A few of the neighbors had gathered on the curb, watching.

Someone touched my shoulder, and I jumped. It was the cop who had grabbed my arm a few minutes before. "Come on, Ellie," he said. "I have to take you in, too."

It felt all wrong that a stranger knew my name. "Can't I just stay here?" I managed to whisper. It was hard to force words out past the empty space in my chest. "I'm sixteen."

He shook his head. "Sorry. We've got orders. Everyone in the house has to go down to the station."

CHAPTER FIVE

They put me in a small, dreary room, square and windowless. It held only a scarred table and two orange plastic chairs. The cop had left me there after promising that "somebody" would be by "soon" to talk to me. There was nothing to read, nothing to look at except the graffiti scratched into the table. With one finger, I traced the deepest of them. It read THE 5-0 ARE SCREWED.

I hadn't even thought to grab my purse, so I didn't have my cell phone. I didn't know who I would call, anyway. Marijean? She wouldn't know what to do any more than I did. Coyote? How could he help me?

At first I did nothing but cry, leaning over to wipe my nose on the knee of my jeans. What was going to happen to me? To my parents? I guessed it could be pretty bad. Finally I forced myself to choke back the tears. I hadn't seen a camera or a tape recorder, and the room didn't have one of those two-way mirrors, but I had seen enough TV to know that someone must be watching me.

After a while, I rested my head on my folded arms and tried to sleep. The best I could manage was a feeling like I was floating, not anchored to anything.

When the door finally opened about three hours later, I

started. Quickly, I composed my face, hoping that the man walking into the room hadn't noticed. I didn't want to look vulnerable or weak. He wore a suit instead of a uniform, but his dirty-blond hair was so short he still looked like a cop or a soldier. He was older, but not as old as Matt, tall and muscular, with fine lines at the corners of his bright blue eyes. In his suit and with his short hair, he looked kind of like the TV father I sometimes daydreamed about.

"Hello, Ellie." He gave me a nod.

I didn't like that he already knew who I was.

"And who are you?" I said.

"I'm Special Agent John Richter. Federal Bureau of Investigation." In one hand, he held a briefcase. With the other, he reached out and shook my hand, squeezing the bones.

Richter sat down in the other chair, set the briefcase on the floor and regarded me calmly. A minute passed. Then another. I looked anywhere else but at him—the floor, a corner where the walls met the ceiling, the toes of my shoes. Whenever I caught a glimpse of Richter's face, he was still studying me. He seemed in no hurry.

Finally, I couldn't take it anymore. "What's going to happen to my parents?"

Richter ignored my question. "What were you doing there, Ellie?"

"What do you mean, what was I doing there? I *live* there." All my anger and fear came boiling up. "I was just doing my homework, like any other kid, and these cops came busting in."

"Only you're not like every other kid, are you, Ellie? The people you live with are drug dealers."

Drug dealers? He can't be serious. "They're *not* drug dealers. Maybe they smoke pot, but that's all." *And maybe they sell it to a few friends. But nothing more than that.*

"And they're not your parents, either, are they? Not your real parents."

"Hey, it doesn't matter who gives birth to you," I said, stung. "They *are* my parents. And they're good parents."

Richter gave an exaggerated sigh. "It's sad, really. We see this all the time. Kids who don't know anything better, so they don't want to leave their lousy homes. But you're going to have to leave, I'm afraid. Unless you're willing to help us."

"What do you mean, leave?"

"With luck, you'll get sent to a foster home. That is, if we can find room in one. At your age, frankly, that's not going to be easy. Babies are one thing, but the number of families who are willing to take in a troubled teen is pretty small. Which means you'll probably go to juvenile hall. You may end up down in Salem if there's not room in Portland."

"But I haven't done anything wrong!" I protested. My eyes stung, and I blinked furiously. *I will not cry, I will not cry, I will not cry.*

"It's for your own good, Ellie. For your own protection."

"Protection?" I had to force the words out. "From what?"

"This atmosphere those people are raising you in. You and their marijuana plants. It's tantamount to abuse to bring up a child in that situation."

This was all such BS. But Richter had the power. Desperate, I snatched at the phrase he had used earlier. "But you said that if I helped you . . . ?"

He looked at me for a long moment. Finally, he nodded, seemingly more to himself than to me. "Tell me about this group of people your parents have been meeting with. The ones who were at your house earlier today. Do you know who those people are, Ellie?"

I shrugged, suddenly glad that I *didn't* know, not really. "They're Mother Earth Defenders. But I don't know their real names. I honestly don't." I wasn't going to tell them that Coyote's name was Ethan, or that he worked at the Multnomah Bike Shop.

Richter leaned toward me, his expression intent. "Tell me this, Ellie, what do you think of their cause?"

"Well, the Earth *is* getting hotter. You know, the glaciers are melting, and there's dead spots in the ocean, and more people are getting skin cancer."

"So how do Mother Earth Defenders stop that?"

I thought about what they'd been discussing at our house. "Protests, petitioning, tree-sits, stuff like that, I guess."

He looked disappointed. "They aren't all peaceful tree-sitters, Ellie. These people are terrorists. Domestic, homegrown terrorists."

"That's ridiculous!" I wasn't that naïve. "They're not flying airplanes into buildings full of people."

Richter slapped his palm on the table, making me jump. "Just because they're Americans doesn't mean they aren't terrorists. Some of the worst terrorists are homegrown. Have you heard of Timothy McVeigh and the Oklahoma City bombing? Some of the Mother Earth Defenders are violent fire bombers who destroy anything they don't approve of. So far, they've been lucky, but we know it's only a matter of time until someone is killed. That's where the FBI comes in. And that's where we need your help."

"Help? What do you mean by help?"

"We need someone who can get inside Mother Earth Defenders."

"No way!" I didn't even need to think. "You'll have to find someone else to do it."

Richter's gaze locked with mine. "We need someone who already has an inside track. Somebody who can find out what they're planning so we can stop it before anyone gets hurt."

"No. No way. I'm not going to be a narc." The thought sickened me. Then I put two and two together. "My parents already turned you down, didn't they?"

He shrugged one shoulder. "We never asked them. MED trusts your parents—but they would never ask them to take part in an action. They're dupes who offer MED a place to meet, maybe a little funding, as well as free, shall we say, refreshments. But they're far too old to be asked to be part of the group. That's why we need someone younger. Someone who can get on the inside and help us gather real evidence."

"No. I can't do it." My eyes felt wet again. "I'd rather go into foster care."

"Let me show you something, Ellie." Richter reached down. As he set his briefcase on his lap and took out a manila envelope, I dashed the tears from my eyes before he could see them. He slid a photo across the table to me.

My eyes traced the lines and shadows of a monochromatic print. I was staring at the charred outlines of a building.

"This was going to be an apartment complex in Southern Oregon for low-income people," Richter said. "That is, until MED set it on fire. Half the valley had to be evacuated when the fire spread to a nearby housing development. And do you know why they set the fire?"

Richter waited until I finally shrugged at his rhetorical question.

"Because they felt it was an environmentally sensitive area. So they burned down the building—and the fire spread to the site they supposedly wanted to protect! That's how MED operates. They burn forest ranger stations because they don't like the Forest Service approving any logging at all, even if it prevents wildfires. They destroy agricultural stations and science labs. In Cannon Beach, they torched a helicopter that sprayed herbicides to fight non-native weeds. Here in Portland, they pipe-bombed a research lab working to make more nutritious rice. But worst of all, we now believe there is a faction of MED that's planning to target people."

With every word he spoke, I kept thinking of Coyote, checking the accusations against the person I knew. "That is so unbelievable. They wouldn't hurt anyone. You should have heard them today. They were talking about freeing *minks*. If they care that much about a mink, they would never hurt a person."

"You don't think so? What if I told you that animals are the only ones they really care about?" He took out another photograph. With a shock, I recognized the yard of my own house. It showed the people who had stayed for dinner the night I had made pasta.

Richter tapped his finger over the picture of Hawk. "This guy here—his real name is Darryl Denigan, by the way—we have e-mails where he says the only way to get people to listen is when their blood is spilled."

I didn't let the expression on my face change, but I remembered how Hawk and Cedar had seemed to disagree when Hawk said that dangerous times called for dangerous measures. "Those e-mails are evidence, then." I crossed my arms. "Use them."

"They're too smart to leave a trail that can be traced back to them. The e-mails are encrypted and anonymous. What we have wouldn't stand up in court."

"I still can't do it." Bile rose in my throat. I didn't want to go into foster care or to juvie, but I couldn't do what he was asking me. Who knew if Richter was even telling the truth?

Richter took back both photographs. "So are you saying you don't care what happens to your parents?"

My parents? "What do you mean?"

"If you don't cooperate with us, Ellie, it's not just a matter of you being put in foster care. Your parents—excuse me, Matt and Laurel—have drug arrests stretching back into the seventies. That makes them career offenders. Career offenders with a grow operation in the basement. And this isn't the seventies anymore, in case they haven't noticed. The law takes drugs a lot more seriously. A lot more. At a minimum, they can be charged with maintaining a dwelling for the purpose of manufacturing marijuana, possession of a controlled substance for the purpose of selling or delivering, felony possession of a schedule II controlled substance, manufacturing marijuana and possession of drug paraphernalia. Not to mention child endangerment."

He paused, but I didn't say anything. The list was overwhelming. Under the table, I clenched my fists so hard I could feel my fingernails cut into my palms. How could my parents have been so stupid?

Richter stood up. "If you help us, we'll make you a deal. We'll drop the charges against your parents for lack of evidence. Otherwise, they will be looking at a long stretch of jail time."

"So if I spy on MED for you, my parents won't have to go to jail? And I won't have to go to a foster home?"

He nodded. "If you help us, we'll help you."

I told myself there was no way that the MEDics could be what Richter said. I thought of Coyote, of how much it had hurt him when his grandfather had shot the deer. *If he got that upset over a deer, he would never do anything to a person. No matter what Richter says, I know Coyote, at least, can't be involved in anything violent.*

So even if I did what Richter asked, probably nothing

would come of it. They wouldn't find anything, and my parents wouldn't get in trouble. Still, I tried to think of another way out, tried to find a place to look other than in Richter's eyes.

But finally I had to speak.

CHAPTER SIX

"We won't tell Matt," Laurel murmured into my hair as she held me close.

Richter had let Laurel in only after I had signed a long form that I had been too exhausted to read. The one detail that caught my attention was that my mother had already signed it. It seemed like a betrayal, but the thought flew from my mind when she pushed passed Richter and hugged me.

It was only after Richter left that I finally allowed my tears to fall. I hadn't let Laurel hug me like this in years, but now I felt like a child again.

When I finally calmed down, I put my lips next to her ear. "They want me to spy for them."

Her reply was no louder than a sigh. "We'll figure out something."

She let go of me and opened the door. I wondered if it had ever been locked. How could I have been so cowed by Richter's threats? In math class, I could solve any problem—why couldn't I have figured out something that would have gotten Richter off my back and saved my parents?

Laurel's plan not to tell Matt was tested right from the beginning. He was waiting for us in the lobby, and as soon as we were on the sidewalk outside the police station, he unleashed a whole bunch of questions. Was I all right? Why were we being released? Had we gotten a lawyer? Had we paid bail?

Laurel held up one hand. "Calm down, Matt," she said in a weary voice. "Nothing bad happened. They were in the middle of questioning me when another cop barged in, and they ended up having this big, angry discussion. It turns out there was a mistake in the warrant."

"What?" Matt looked dazed.

"It wouldn't have held up in court. And I started telling them about how we have a friend who's a lawyer—you know, that guy Mike Callinan at Legal Aid—and about how he could sue their asses, and suddenly they decided the best thing was to let us go. Act like it never happened."

Laurel went on, constructing her lie in midair, adding more details about how the police had apologized, until her story seemed more real than what had happened. The more Laurel talked, the less Matt seemed to listen. It was like he just checked out.

Because the cops had taken us away, we had to call a taxi to get home. Crammed next to him in the backseat, I looked at Matt whenever I thought he wouldn't notice. In his shadowed eyes, I saw how exhausted he was. Exhausted and old and scared. And that scared me more than Richter had.

When we got home, there was no marijuana growing in our basement anymore. The only clue the plants had ever been there was the metal tracks on the ceiling where the grow lights had run. The house had been thoroughly searched, but the only stuff missing had to do with my parents' pot.

That didn't mean everything wasn't a mess. Closets and

cupboards had been flung wide open. Everyone's dresser drawers gaped, even mine. Grossed out by the idea of some pervy cop rifling through my underwear, I dumped the entire contents of the drawer in my laundry basket and carried it to the washing machine.

When I walked past my parents' room, I saw Matt lying on his back on the bed, his eyes closed. His arms were by his sides, and he was absolutely still. When I was thirteen, Matt had had a heart attack. So I stood for a long moment in the doorway, watching to make sure his chest still rose and fell. My head felt like it might split in two. How could my parents have been so selfish?

In the kitchen, I found Laurel. She was making a stir-fry. It was nearly ten o'clock at night, but it was like she was pretending it was still dinnertime, that nothing had happened.

"What am I going to do now?" I said. My voice was hard and harsh.

Laurel put down her chef's knife and put her finger to her lips. "Shh! I don't want Matt to hear us."

"I don't want to do this," I said. My voice wasn't much softer than it had been before.

She tried to put her arms around me again. For a second, I wanted to close my eyes and lean into her soft warmth. But I wasn't a kid anymore. And it was Laurel and Matt who had gotten me into this mess, with their stupid reluctance to admit that it was no longer 1972. I shook off her hands and took a step back.

"How could you do this to me?" I crossed my arms.

"We didn't do it to you. The Man did." I heard the capital letters in Laurel's voice, as if she were speaking about a real person.

"For once, couldn't you have done what 'the Man' said? Couldn't you follow the rules?"

"Even when the rules don't make any sense?" Her tired eyes pleaded with me. "In a lot of countries, pot's legal. Cigarettes are a lot more harmful."

"But we don't live in other countries, *Mom*," I said sarcastically, watching her flinch. "We live here. Where it's not legal and where they can use it as an excuse to get the MEDics."

"Look, we'll figure out something," Laurel said again, turning away to slide some chopped onions into the wok. "But our first priority is to keep Matt out of jail. He couldn't hack it, not at his age. With his heart, and the sentences they give out now, he could even *die* there. You saw how bad he looks tonight. I want him to call his cardiologist, but he won't."

Laurel picked up her knife again. "Besides, it's the lesser of two evils. Whatever the MEDics are, it's up to them to prove it. If Richter is wrong and they aren't turning to violence, he promised me they would drop the investigation."

"But what if he's right?" I had to ask. "If he's right, then what?"

"Then," Laurel said as she brought her butcher knife down with a thwack on the green tops of a bunch of carrots, "then they've made their bed. And they'll have to lie in it."

That night, I couldn't sleep. I kept thinking about what Richter had said. So I got up and Googled MED. One article said that MED was "dedicated to taking the motive out of environmental destruction by causing economic damage to businesses." But most of what I found called them ecoterrorists.

In Oregon alone, MED had claimed responsibility for seven "actions" since September. Like Richter had said, they had firebombed a helicopter used to spray weeds, as well as burned down a wild horse corral, a logging truck and a ranger's station, for a total of more than five million dollars in damages.

I also read about a reporter who had infiltrated a group of MEDics in England. After he published a series of stories about them, he had been abducted by four masked men. They let him go—after branding the letters *M-E-D* on his back.

I went back to bed, but just tossed and turned until the sheets were wrapped suffocatingly tight around my body. I kept trying to think of a way out, but found none.

In the morning, Matt, who was usually up early, stayed in bed. Bustling about the kitchen as if nothing had happened the night before, Laurel made me oatmeal for breakfast. She set it down before me, and it was just the way I liked it—with lots of maple syrup, raisins and almonds. I ate two spoonfuls, but when I tried to swallow a third one, it wouldn't go down. I barely made it to the bathroom before I threw up in the sink. When I lifted my head, my eyes looked like two bruises in the mirror.

At school, I didn't hear a thing the teachers said that day. My head ached, and I kept my eyes down so no one would call on me.

When the last bell rang, I met Marijean outside the front doors. For the first time that year, I was glad that we didn't have a single class together. Because as soon as she looked at me, Marijean knew something was up.

"What's wrong? You look terrible."

"Nothing." I couldn't tell her the truth. I couldn't tell anyone.

"It's something to do with Coyote, isn't it? Did he call you? Is it that other girl?"

"What other girl?" I barely heard her.

"The one with the red dreads."

"No, it's not that." I tried to find something to say that wasn't a complete lie. "It's my dad. His heart was acting up again last night. He wouldn't call the doctor, but he looked terrible."

"Oh." Marijean hugged me, then reached in her pack for her cigarettes.

I held out my hand. "Can I have one?"

"What?" She raised her eyebrows in surprise. "But you don't ever smoke. You're always telling me how bad it is for you."

"Just give me one, okay?" Smoking *was* bad, which was why it was suddenly so appealing. Smoking would match how I felt inside.

"I'm just saying." She put two in her mouth, lit them both with her lighter and handed one to me.

I took a deep drag, welcoming how it burned my throat, and then I started coughing. As I coughed and coughed, I imagined the smoke turning my lungs all gray and dirty, the way I felt.

That Saturday, I walked over to Multnomah Village to meet Coyote as we had planned. On any other day, my footsteps might have been slowed by nervousness. Now it felt like every step took me closer to the edge of a cliff.

I had barely stepped into the doorway of the bike store when Coyote ducked under the counter. "I'm leaving, George!" he called over his shoulder.

George was in the back, holding a small wrench between his teeth. He grunted in response.

Coyote grabbed two tall mugs. I tried to smile at him, but my face felt stiff.

He held the door open for me. "Hey, I like your bag."

My messenger bag was made of green fabric patterned with sky-blue scribbles. Before I bought the fabric at the Bins, it had been a tablecloth. "Thanks. I made it." The fact that Coyote noticed small things about me made me feel worse. I wondered if he had noticed that today I wasn't wearing any eyeliner. My face felt oddly bare without it. But I figured wearing makeup was fundamentally incompatible with being a MEDic.

When we got a block away from Village Coffee, Coyote didn't say anything, just flashed one of his mended-toothed grins and sprinted ahead of me. I stood there for a second, trying to figure out what he was doing. By the time I finally started running myself, it was too late. When I got to the counter, he was already handing over a bill to the barista.

"Hey," I said, panting, "I thought I said next time it would be my treat!"

He shrugged one shoulder, trying hard not to look pleased with himself. "I was here first."

The barista handed Coyote back one of his mugs, which Coyote then handed to me. "Twelve-ounce nonfat latte with a double shot, right?"

"Right." I forced an even bigger smile onto my face. "Hey, it's such a nice day—can we sit outside?" I didn't want anyone to overhear us.

"Sure." Coyote picked up his cup of tea. We went outside and sat at one of the two small, round tables on the sidewalk. He petted a yellow Labrador retriever tied to a parking sign.

"So how's work going?" I asked, casting about for a neutral topic. I wasn't sure how to get started.

"It's real busy now." He spread his grease-stained fingers out and regarded them. The nail on his right thumb was bruised. "Everyone's getting ready for summer."

"Do you like working there?"

"It's pretty good. George is easy to work for. And I like working with my hands." He took a sip of tea. "How are things going at school?"

"Okay." Since the arrest, I had gotten a D on one quiz and a C-minus on the other. "In English, we're reading *Othello*."

"That's the one where Othello thinks his wife is cheating on him, right?" I must have looked surprised, because Coyote said, "Just because I got my GED doesn't mean I don't like to read."

"Yeah, Iago sets her up so she looks guilty." That made me think of Richter. The coffee turned to acid in my stomach. I tried to ignore it and changed the subject. "Thanks for bringing the extra cup for me. Were you no longer willing to underwrite my profligate use of natural resources?"

He grinned. "Oh, you're already damned to hell." He took a sip of his tea, and when he looked up again, his face was serious. "Besides, if we don't start doing things differently, it will be too late. That's why I'm part of"—he hesitated—"that group."

I took a deep breath. "That's what I wanted to talk to you about. Can I be part of it, too?"

"Do you really know what you're asking? It's not a commitment you can make lightly."

Even though we were the only ones on the sidewalk, I lowered my voice. "You mean because you guys sometimes do things that are against the law, like freeing the minks? Well, I think there's a higher law."

He looked up from his tea, and I forced my eyes not to waver from his green gaze. "It's fine to talk about higher law, but some of the stuff we do"—he lowered his voice even further—"means we might end up going to jail. And if you get caught, being a MEDic means no plea bargains, no deals, no selling out your friends."

I didn't drop my gaze. "You heard what Matt said. My parents brought me up to believe in fighting for what's important."

"Sorry, we just have to be cautious," Coyote said. "Not everyone supports what we do like your parents. They get it. Even if they are a little too old and a little too mainstream to be MEDics, they still get it."

Normally I would have smiled at the idea that anyone thought my parents were mainstream. Instead, I just took another sip of my bitter coffee.

Coyote stared at his tea for a long time. And then he said, "Let me talk to Cedar. We might be able to use you."

I nodded and pretended to smile. But inside, I was dying.

CHAPTER NINE

"So why do you want to join us?" Cedar asked. His face was unsmiling, all angles and planes.

I was sitting with nine MEDics around a long picnic bench in a rundown park in North Portland. The sun was out, but we were the only ones at this end of the park. At the far end, some guys played basketball. They had tried to sell us dope when we walked by.

Even though I was with the MEDics, it was clear that I wasn't part of the group. The only good thing was that Coyote was next to me. I wondered if he felt how my whole body trembled. Of the other people at the table, Hawk, Liberty and Meadow seemed openly hostile. Blue, on the other hand, gave me a thumbs-up when we first met in the parking lot. Even Jack Rabbit and Seed had smiled at me, although a little furtively. It was harder to tell what Grizz was thinking. And with Cedar, it was impossible. I wondered if he ever smiled.

I noticed Cedar hadn't used the word MED. Probably playing it safe. Before we sat down, he had asked Liberty to frisk me. She hadn't held anything back, either, her red dreads brushing against me as she ran her hands firmly down my legs and then up again, under my long denim skirt. The park was the kind of place where even frisking someone didn't draw any attention.

I took a deep breath. If I could convince Cedar, then the others would fall in line. "If we don't act now, it will be too late to save the Earth. It's going to take more than recycling newspapers and reusing plastic bags. I want to be part of a group that's actually doing something real." Although my voice was confident, under the table my legs wouldn't stop shaking. I prayed that no one else noticed.

"This isn't a social club, you know," Liberty said. Her lips thinned down to a line. "It's a serious group. It's not all filled with—with cheerleaders." She spit out the word.

I got a quick vision of her in whatever high school she went to, dissed by the popular kids. Liberty must be way on the outer edge if she thought anyone would mistake me for a cheerleader. I gave her my best cold stare. "You heard what my parents said. I've been around protests all my life."

"This is more than protests." Meadow shook her head. "And this isn't like joining a book club or the Girl Scouts."

"Hey, I'm just as serious about this as you are," I objected. *Serious as a heart attack.*

"Probably more serious. *She's* not rebelling against her parents," Coyote said. "She's not just doing this to get a rise out of somebody."

His words had seemed aimed at Meadow, but it was Liberty whose cheeks turned the color of her hair. "She can't just say she wants to be a member and waltz right in," she said.

I sighed loudly. I was tired of people telling me what I couldn't do. "Fine. What do I need to do?"

Grizz shifted in his seat and said, "Look, Ellie, okay, you have to prove yourself? Same as the rest of us?"

It was hard to tell behind his huge beard, but his expression seemed friendly. Looking at him, I started to feel like I might actually be able to carry this thing off. "How do I do that?"

Hawk said, "You have to pick a target, do an action by yourself and get away without being caught." With his big, bulging eyes set in his bony face, he reminded me of some kind of insect. "You have to prove you are committed."

By myself? I had thought if I had to do anything, it would be as part of the group, not acting on my own. I bit the inside of my cheek. *It's for Matt,* I reminded myself.

"If that's what I need to do, I'll do it." I tried to keep my voice steady.

"Are you sure?" Blue asked from the far side of the table. Her blue eyes were gentle. "Because it's fine to be a supporter. Not everyone can get involved at the same level."

"I'm sure," I said. "This is something I believe in. If we don't act now, the Earth will die."

Cedar looked at me thoughtfully for a long moment, then nodded his approval. And almost as an aside he added, "Oh, and you'll need to bring us proof."

"To be honest, Cedar kind of scares me," I whispered to Coyote. We were sitting in the back of a nearly empty TriMet bus, going home after the meeting. "Does he ever smile?"

Coyote shot me a sideways grin. "And risk damaging his reputation?" Then he turned serious. "Cedar has been at this longer than any of us, and he has more to lose. About five years ago, he served two years in jail for an action. They offered him a deal if he would give up the others—and he wouldn't. But staying involved in MED means that he risks more than any of the rest of us. That's why he wants to make sure anyone who wants to join is committed."

Before the meeting had broken up, Cedar had explained to me that I had to pick a target, plan an action, take a photograph of myself there and then bring it back as proof. The photograph would not only get me in—it would also give the group leverage over me. It would prove that I was already guilty of a crime before I even joined MED.

"Okay, let me give you some advice," Coyote said. "Don't pick something in your neighborhood, and don't buy the supplies there, either. It probably sounds like overkill, but these are the kinds of things that have tripped people up in the past."

"But what should I hit?" Saying "hit" made me feel like an actor in a bad movie. This couldn't be real.

"Get out the yellow pages and take your pick. Golf courses, butcher shops, animal research facilities, SUV dealerships. Except you should start small. Bigger actions require more people and more planning."

"What have other MEDics hit?"

"Well, a lot of people have picked McDonald's because they generate so much trash and are destroying rain forests to plant soybeans to feed their chickens."

"That sounds good." My parents had raised me to hate McDonald's, so I didn't even have a moral issue with the idea. I imagined myself lobbing a firebomb through a McDonald's window one night and running like hell.

Coyote turned practical. "But the problem is that a lot of them are open half the night, or have prep or cleanup staff there. You might want to target something quieter."

The bus stopped and let off an old man who had been sitting by the driver. Now we were the only passengers left. Still, I waited until we were rumbling down the street again before I asked my next question. "What was *your* first target?"

He looked sheepish. "A Mickey D's, actually. Glued the locks. And nearly got caught by the prep cook."

"Glued the locks?" I thought MED had been asking me to do something more dramatic than squirting glue in a lock.

"Look, even if all you do is glue the locks closed, it still accomplishes a lot." Coyote sounded a little defensive.

"How?"

"One, it makes them realize how vulnerable they are. Two, they can't do any business as long as no one can get in. Three, they'll have to call a locksmith, and those aren't cheap. And it's quick and easy. It takes less than one minute to glue the locks if you do it right. So with only one person, one minute and less than ten dollars' worth of supplies, you can disrupt the whole apparatus."

"One minute?" I echoed. That didn't sound that bad. I reached past him to ring the bell for my stop, bringing my face dangerously close to his. Suddenly, I wanted to kiss him, which was the stupidest thing. How could I want to kiss someone I was planning on selling out to the FBI? I sat back in my seat and tried to compose myself.

Coyote half turned, so that he was even closer to me than

before. "You know, when you asked about joining us, at first I thought it was a bad idea."

"Why?" I struggled to keep my expression neutral.

"You're younger than the rest of us. I thought maybe it was more your parents' idea than yours. But now I know it was because *you* wanted it. And I'm glad. I wouldn't want to have to keep secrets from you, Ellie." He leaned even closer, and I caught my breath.

"Thirty-fifth Avenue," the bus driver called out. I saw him staring at us in the rearview mirror. I hadn't even realized the bus had stopped.

"Oops, this is me," I said hurriedly. I got up and grabbed my backpack. "I'll call you as soon as it's over."

As I walked up my driveway, I saw Matt and Laurel through the kitchen window. They were both laughing at something. My eyes filled with angry tears. The only reason they were safe and sound was because of what I was doing. And to do it, I was going to have to betray Coyote and his friends.

CHAPTER TEN

The Saturday before my action was scheduled, I was supposed to be writing a report on how European colonization was still affecting countries today. But instead I just stared out the window, wondering how I could get myself out of the mess my parents had made.

I jumped when my cell phone began to vibrate across my desk. It was Marijean.

"What are you doing?" she asked.

Hearing her voice made me feel guilty. Marijean and I had been friends so long that we knew each other inside and out. Which was exactly why I had been avoiding her.

"Working on that paper for history."

"Do you want to come over and work on it here?"

"No, I should stay here and concentrate. I didn't do that great on the last test, and stupid Tamson said if I didn't get an A on this paper, I might get a C for the whole class." I had never gotten a C in anything before.

"A C?" Marijean echoed, stunned. She was a B or C or sometimes even a D student, not because she wasn't smart, but because she didn't care that much. But she knew that I cared. "Ellie, what's wrong with you? Is it your dad? Is it Coyote?"

"I don't know." It was all of them, but of course I couldn't explain. "Maybe I have spring fever. I'm just kind of not myself these days."

The pause on the other end of the phone was so long I thought for a second that the call might have been dropped. Then she said, "Are you mad at me?"

"No!" I tried to reassure her. "It's just that I've had a lot of things on my mind. And you're right. I'm worried about my dad, and I'm not sure where things are going with Coyote. I like him a lot, but I think he just sees me as a friend. He's really nice to me—but he's really nice to everyone."

"Well, don't forget your other friends," Marijean said softly. "I'm always here if you want to talk."

She was clearly hurt, but I told myself I was doing her a favor keeping her in the dark. I would go back to being Marijean's best friend as soon as this whole thing was over.

After we hung up, I gave up on my paper. Maybe I would work on it later. Besides, what difference would a C really make? A C was the least of my troubles. So I got on the bus and went across the river to the Bins. If I kept myself busy, maybe I wouldn't spend as much time worrying.

The Bins was called that because it was full of bins, and each of *them* was full of unorganized and unwashed goods. The place had a fake-strawberry smell, some weird fragrance/disinfectant that couldn't quite overcome the cumulatively nauseating stench of thousands of used items. The worst were the preworn shoes.

But the upside was that everything—coats, sweaters, socks, pillowcases, scarves—cost just ninety-nine cents a pound.

I had just picked up an interesting-looking square of blue-and-yellow waterproof fabric—it might have once been a tablecloth, although a foot-wide circle had inexplicably been cut out of the middle—when I saw Blue enter the store. She walked over to the nearest bin and picked up a bolt of faded red velvet. She had half unrolled it and was running her hands over it when she noticed me. A smile lit up her face. Picking up the bolt, she walked over.

I couldn't help but smile back. And it was a relief, in a way, to see her. With Blue, I only had to pretend halfway.

"Looking for something special?" Blue asked, with a meaningful lift to her voice. Coyote had briefed me on the fine points on what to wear to an action. You wore dark clothes, but not head-to-toe black, because that was too obvious. You bought shoes that were two or three sizes too big and stuffed the toes with newspaper, so the cops wouldn't be able to trace you through any footprints you left behind. You wore a sweatshirt or sweater on top of another top in a completely different color and took the top layer off as soon as you were done. That way any potential witness would give a misleading description of who the police should be on the lookout for.

"Actually, I make stuff," I said. "Like this sweater." It had begun life as an unadorned teal-blue cardigan, but now it had appliquéd four-petaled felt flowers—grass green, sky blue and bright fuchsia. The stems were embroidered with fuzzy purple yarn.

"Nice," she said. "I make stuff, too."

She was wearing the same clothes she had in my parents' living room, black Cahartt overalls and a plain olive-green T-shirt. I could not imagine Blue wearing red velvet anything.

"Furniture, not clothes," she said, reading my look. "It's how I make my living, actually. I get on my bike every morning and ride up and down the streets of Portland, looking for reject furniture people have put out on the curb for the garbageman. I know all the trash routes in a twenty-mile radius."

"What do you do once you find something?" I asked. "Sand it and paint it?"

"That's only the beginning. Have you got a minute? Because I live near here and I could show you."

Before we left, I bought the tablecloth, two sweaters, a pair of jeans and a hooded sweatshirt for a dollar ninety-eight. Blue looked at the dark sweatshirt and jeans and gave me a knowing smile. Her own fabric set her back nearly twelve bucks, which was lot at the Bins. Once we were outside, she unlocked her bicycle and rolled it home next to me, while I carried both of our purchases.

"So have you decided on your action?" Blue asked once we reached an empty stretch of sidewalk where no one could overhear us.

"Yeah. The Federal Predator Control Office."

"Why did you pick that place?"

"Because *something* in Oregon should still be left wild." I had read on the Internet that Federal wildlife agents shot, trapped or poisoned more than 1.6 million animals a year—all because they were considered a threat to livestock, crops or travel. Another, more basic reason was that the Federal Predator Control Office was on a quiet street and no one would be in the building in the middle of the night.

Blue nodded thoughtfully. Her expression lightened as she stopped in front of a tiny house with a detached ramshackle garage that looked like an afterthought. "We're home. The house was built in 1911, but the garage came along about ten years later, when they figured out cars weren't a fad."

She took a ring of keys from her pocket and unlocked the huge, rusty padlock. Instead of a roll-up door, the garage had two doors that swung out like a giant cupboard. Inside were more than a dozen pieces of furniture, including a battered desk, a small wooden table, a dresser that had been painted hot pink decades ago and old windows with hinges still attached. There were parts of furniture, too. I saw random table and chair legs, a column and a couple of lengths of molding.

"This is pretty cool," I said, leaning down to look at a cherub's head.

"I like castaways," she said. She pulled out an old upholstered chair with claw feet, arms turned out like wings and a back that spread like a fan. It looked like animals had been eating and/or living in it. And it smelled like they had been peeing on it, too. Blue didn't seem fazed. "I'm going to tear this down to the wood and springs and reupholster it with this fabric."

"Wow," I said as she took the bolt of velvet from my arms. "This makes what I do with clothes look like nothing. How do you know how to do all those things?"

She shrugged. "I just figured it out. After all, if I make a mistake, I'm not out very much. And I never try to make it look new. That would be boring. Like, I'm going to turn that window into a series of picture frames, but I'll leave the hinges on. It's like a reminder of what something used to be."

I nodded. I could already see the window through her eyes.

"It takes garbage out of the landfill and gives people something that they like. I'm hoping that people will look at my stuff and realize that you don't need to throw everything away. It's surprising what you see if you just keep your eyes open." From a shelf, Blue pulled down an open shoe box filled with plastic bags. "Want to see some of my finds?"

She put the box on an old wooden table and began spreading out her treasures: a detailed Art Deco hinge, vintage typewriter keys, pale-pink and baby-blue doorknobs and a colorful bag of broken glass.

"What's that for?" I asked. The glass was a jumble of colors—mostly green, but also red, yellow and blue.

"I'm going to make a mosaic for a tabletop."

"Didn't you cut yourself picking it up?"

She shrugged. "Not too badly. Sometimes you have to be willing to put your own safety at risk for the greater good." Her expression was serious. Clearly, Blue wasn't just talking about a mosaic tabletop. I made myself meet her gaze. Much as I was starting to like Blue, I had to be fake with her, too, so she wouldn't doubt my sincerity. After a long second, I asked, "How do you carry some of the heavy stuff home on your bike?"

"Oh, I've gotten pretty good at balancing stuff. But I've also got an old car. That orange Volvo parked on the street. Yesterday I brought home that dresser strapped on top."

"What do you do with this stuff when you're done?" I ran my hand across the battered surface of the dresser.

"I sell it at a consignment store downtown. They call it shabby chic." She winked as if she was putting something over on them. "Sometimes I give it to friends."

I wondered if Blue thought of me as a friend. Part of me wished she did. But another part of me wondered what she would think of me if she really knew everything.

I just hoped she never found out.

ELEVEN

At 1:17 A.M. on Wednesday, I walked down a sidewalk in Southeast Portland. Two blocks away was a brightly lit 7-Eleven, but all the other businesses along the street were closed.

Dressed in the dark clothes from the Bins, I had never felt more conspicuous in my life. Why would someone be out at this time of night and on foot? I just hoped no one could tell I was a girl. If people knew you were a girl wandering around in the middle of the night, it opened up to a whole new set of problems.

My heart was beating as fast as if I had been running. But I wasn't supposed to run; I wasn't supposed to draw attention to myself. I tried to remember the things Coyote had told me: to plan what to say if a cop or security guy spotted me, to have at least two exit strategies mapped out, to strip off my top layer as soon as I could after I was finished.

I was also supposed to assume that a camera was following my every move, even if I couldn't see one. That's why my hood was pulled up. It made a little cave, and in it my breathing echoed, too fast and too shallow. I was freaking out, even though I had made a dry run two nights ago. Real MEDics made dry runs. Real MEDics cased their targets. Real MEDics were professionals.

Tonight, I was fully aware that I was only pretending to be a MEDic.

The street was so quiet that my footsteps echoed down the block. My eyes scanned the area, but I was too anxious to tell if anything looked different from when I had done my dry runs. In my pocket was a tube of glue with BBs mixed in. Coyote had explained that, combined with glue, the BBs would make the building's locks impenetrable.

The two-story building was dark inside. Through the gold lettering on the old-fashioned, wood-trimmed glass door, I could just make out a counter, with two desks in the shadows beyond it. The lock was inside the doorknob. I looked both ways. The street was deserted. As I pulled the tube of glue free, I stepped close to the door, shielding the knob with my body. One more look around. I was still alone. I inserted the tip of the tube into the lock and squeezed until I felt resistance. When I pulled back the tube, a drop of glue oozed from the lock.

I took out the cheapest, reddest lipstick I had been able to find at Target. As fast as possible, I scrawled **THE MEDICS ARE WATCHING**! on the glass of the door, one word per line, writing over the gold letters that were already there. I even used my left hand so the handwriting couldn't be matched up with me later. Then I pulled out Matt's digital camera, held it out at arm's length and snapped a picture of me and the door. The flash made me flinch. No matter how bad the quality was, it would have to be proof enough. I put the camera in my pocket and started walking rapidly down the street.

"Hey, kid! What are you doing?"

I jumped about a foot, then looked back. Through the open window of an old, metallic green car slowly moving down the street, a bald guy with a cigarette between his lips was staring at me.

Immediately forgetting all I had been taught, I ran. The rumble of the car's engine speeded up. My two escape routes both led to a MAX station a couple of blocks away, where a train was due in seven minutes. But waiting at the station, I would be too easy to find. I needed a new getaway plan. I risked a look behind me. The car was only about forty feet away.

Crap! I had to lose him. But how? At the end of the block, I darted around the corner and put on an even bigger burst of speed, trying to get to the end of the next block so that I could cut right or left before he came around the corner. Maybe I could make turns faster than he could follow.

But the low growl of his engine was right behind me, his headlights illuminating the street.

There! A narrow, dark passage between a bar and a shuttered store. On the far side, I saw the soft glow of a streetlight. It looked like the passageway ran all the way back to the street behind. I hurried down it, praying my black sweatshirt would blend into the shadows.

Wham! I crashed into a metal gate. If I hadn't had my hands outstretched, I would have hit it face-first. Behind me, I heard the car slow to a stop, then a rusty car door creaking open.

The gate was about seven feet tall, but there weren't any spikes on top. I spied a blue rubber garbage can and dragged it over. Holding on to the bars, I managed to clamber onto the garbage can and then over the top of the gate. I put one leg over just as the plastic lid of the garbage can gave way. With a sideways lurch, I tumbled over the gate, landing hard on my shoulder and hip. Even though it hurt to move, I got up immediately and half ran, half limped away down the alley.

"Come back here, kid!" the man shouted behind me. I heard his footsteps stop at the gate. I expected to hear him trying to vault over the fence himself, but apparently he wasn't willing to risk it.

As soon as I was around the corner, I yanked off my black sweatshirt. Underneath I had on an orange T-shirt. The sweatshirt got tossed in the first Dumpster I passed. The lipstick went into a second, and the glue into a third. Every time I came to an intersection, I picked the street that looked the darkest and most deserted.

I ran when I could, but had to stop and walk more and more as I got tired. My breath came in gasps, and my hip and shoulder ached. I walked across the Steel Bridge into downtown, but it was too dark to see the river below. Finally, I made it to the bus mall. At that time of night, it was only me and a few homeless guys muttering to themselves. Luckily, they didn't try to talk to me before the bus finally came forty-five minutes later.

It was after three in the morning when I finally walked up my driveway. It was hard to put one foot in front of the other. My legs felt heavy as lead, and my hip was throbbing. I couldn't wait to take a warm shower and crawl into bed.

I turned the key in the lock and eased myself in the front

door. As I walked through the living room, I jumped, the last bit of adrenaline I had jolting through my veins. Laurel was sitting in Matt's recliner, dressed in a long, white nightgown, her iron-gray hair loose down her back. I had told her earlier in the day that I would be out late, without spelling out it was for MED. But she must have guessed, and now here she was.

Without a word, Laurel stood up and held her arms out to me. She had put me in this position, and now she wanted to hold me? I pushed past her, shaking off her hand when she tried to touch me. "I'm going to bed," I said, in a voice that made it clear that I didn't want to be bothered by her.

As I entered the hall, I heard a small, strangled noise. Turning, I saw the shine of tear tracks on her cheeks. My mother, crying?

"I'm sorry, honey, so sorry," she choked out. I noticed she kept her voice low, so she could still keep Matt in the dark. "This is all our fault."

"You know what, Mom?" I said. "I don't care if you're sorry. It's too late for that." I went into my room, but instead of slamming the door, I closed it very, very gently.

CHAPTER TWELVE

"Did anyone see you?" Cedar asked. It was three days later, and the MEDics were passing around the blurry photo I had taken. We were back on the picnic bench in the same rundown park we had met in earlier. Coyote sat next to Cedar, and just his presence eased a little of my nervousness.

I wasn't sure how to answer Cedar's question. The paper had never run a story about the glued lock, much less that there had been a witness. Under the table, Blue, who was sitting next to me, patted my knee.

Liberty watched me, her face alert. Meadow chewed her thumbnail, looking at me from underneath her bangs. Hawk stared at me with his creepy pop-out eyes, expressionless. The others seemed to take it for granted that I was already in. Jack Rabbit had high-fived me when I arrived, and Grizz had given me a hug that lifted me off my feet.

I thought about lying, but what if Cedar had had someone watching me? If this was some kind of final test, I didn't want to screw it up. "A guy saw me after I was done, but I took evasive action." I tried to sound professional.

"How do you know you weren't followed?" Liberty demanded. "How do we know you haven't compromised us all?"

She looked around, as if expecting the others to chime in, but no one else said anything.

"Because I lost him," I said. "Besides, when he yelled at me, he called me 'kid.' I'm pretty sure he thought I was a guy. And I was far away and had my hood pulled up."

Cedar looked at me for a long time, expressionless. Finally, he nodded and said, "You did well."

I let out my breath. "So I'm in?"

For an answer, Blue clapped her hands and asked, "What would you like your MED name to be?"

Everyone turned to me, waiting for an answer. But I didn't want to surrender Ellie.

"How about something for the color of your eyes?" Coyote suggested. "Of course, Blue's taken, but you could be Ocean. Or Lake. Or Sky."

"Sky," I said, trying it on for size. And then more confidently. "Sky. I like that."

"All right, Sky," Hawk said. "We have another mission for you. Do you know where the Hummer dealership is in Beaverton?"

MOTHER EARTH DEFENDERS— CLAIM FOR HUMMER ARSON

Symbolizing consumer decadence at its worst,
$1 million worth of Hummers were torched last night in
Beaverton. The firebombing of the Beaverton Hummer
dealership was meant to punish carmakers and consumers
for their love affairs with these shamelessly gas-guzzling
behemoths that destroy everything they encounter. They are
a status symbol for rich American consumers, who are killing
more people on this planet than anyone else. Sucking the
land dry, these oversized toys are at the forefront of this vile,
imperialistic culture's caravan toward self-destruction.
We can no longer allow the rich to parade around in their
armored existence, leaving a wasteland behind in their tire
tracks. The time is right to fight back.
We must strike out against what destroys us before we
choke to death on smog or are silenced by the state.

Take the power into your own hands.
It's your life.

THIRTEEN

It had been four days since we had set the fire at the Hummer dealership. Four days since Coyote had dropped me off at my house and then taken Meadow home. Four days of longing to see Coyote, knowing that I couldn't see him or even call him. The MEDics had made it clear we must all avoid contact after an action, stick to our everyday routines.

At night, I slept in snatches, waking from dreams where I tripped and the fire consumed me, or an explosion sent my body cartwheeling through the air.

Without having any idea of my involvement, Matt talked to Laurel about the fire at the Hummer dealership, speaking obliquely about "our friends." The night after the Hummer action, Laurel had come into my room to wish me good night. She leaned down to kiss me on the forehead, which she hadn't done since I was in grade school. I thought about turning my head away, but instead I just closed my eyes while her cool lips briefly touched my skin. Something about the tears I had seen the night of my first action had been eating at me. I knew she was sorry.

When my parents weren't around, I compulsively checked news sites. The FBI must have known who was behind it, known all our names and exactly where to find us, but they fed the media a different story, one in which the fire had burned up any clues and they were completely in the dark.

I wondered how the FBI really felt about what happened. Gluing locks was one thing, but I didn't think they had wanted me to cause a million dollars' worth of damage.

Then Agent Richter left a message on my cell phone, asking me to meet him in a service hallway at the Washington Square Mall.

Inside the mall, I walked past the drinking fountain, past the doors for the restrooms. At the end of the hall, I turned to look at the streams of shoppers shuffling by. They seemed like zombies, hypnotized by all the choices. My end of the hallway was shadowed, with unmarked doors on either side.

I had the creepy feeling that I was invisible.

I knocked three times on the second door on the left, just as Richter had instructed me to. He half opened the door, I slipped inside and he closed it behind me. He gave me a tired smile that did nothing to ease my anxiety. The long, narrow room seemed to be a storeroom for mall decorations, with boxes labeled XMAS LIGHTS AND HALLOWEEN SKELETONS. The animatronic bear I had been photographed with every Christmas when I was little was probably in here someplace.

"I don't like this," I said as Richter leaned against a box marked CORNUCOPIA. "I don't like this at all."

"Why?" He seemed genuinely surprised.

"You wanted me to prove myself. I thought it would be

something little. Not . . ." My voice faltered as I thought again of the fire.

"You did exactly what we wanted you to do, and you did it well," Richter said.

"Better than we expected." The new voice made me jump.

I turned to face the new speaker, who had appeared from behind a pile of boxes. Dressed in jeans and an old Pendleton shirt, he looked like one of my parents' friends. His grizzled hair was caught back in a thin ponytail, as if his ability to grow hair on the back of his head made up for the receding hairline in front.

"Who are you?" For a second I wondered if there were people behind every pile of boxes. Was I being watched? Was this being videotaped? Anything seemed possible.

He regarded me calmly. "A friend."

"Do you have a name?"

He shrugged. "You can call me anything you want."

Richter nodded like it was okay. But it wasn't okay. What had I gotten myself into?

Deciding to ignore Ponytail, I turned back to Richter. "How can you say that I did a good job?" I protested. "That fire caused a million dollars' worth of damage."

"Gluing locks was something anyone could do. Torching that car dealership was your first real test. They know you're willing to go all the way. They'll trust you more now. You helped them create something that got them headlines across the nation."

I snorted in frustration. "Helped them create something?

Because of what I did—something *you* wanted me to do—this guy got his car lot burned down. All I did was help them destroy a million dollars' worth of cars."

"He has insurance," Ponytail said dismissively. "I hear he might even be claiming a few things burned up that didn't. And the day after the fire, he even sold two Hummers from the far end of the lot." He gave me a mirthless grin. "You should tell those MEDic people that they got it bass-ackwards. That fire put tons of pollution into the air, and putting it out meant a bunch of dirty water went straight into the river and then the ocean."

His words just made my head hurt even more.

Richter touched my arm. "Look, if you hadn't lit the match, someone else would have. Remember, our priority is to stop them before they *kill* someone. And by getting even deeper inside, now you'll be able to help us do that."

"But why do you need me? I've been doing some reading about MED. It's just a bunch of independent groups—you'll only ever know about what's happening in this one."

"Cedar's group is willing to go a lot farther than most," Richter said matter-of-factly. "More than just pickets and protests. They're willing to destroy to make their point. It's only a matter of time until they turn to violence. Have you heard them talk about anything like that at all—even if it's just a hint?"

I shook my head. "I can tell there are still things they don't talk about in front of me. But hurting somebody, it really doesn't seem like something they would do."

"Did you know that a cleaning woman was scheduled to be in the car dealership office the next night?" Ponytail asked. "What if she had gotten caught in the fire?"

The hair on my arms rose. "But Coyote and I staked it out."

"Staked it out?" Ponytail echoed sarcastically. "Dropping by for a couple of hours for a night or two doesn't count as professional surveillance."

I shivered. Had they followed us?

"If you can tell me everything that happened, why do you even need me, anyway?" I said, taking a step toward the door.

Richter grabbed my wrist. "We do need you. We can't always follow them, not without their knowing it. We need to be able to stop them before somebody gets killed. Not come in when it's too late and mop up the blood."

I shook myself free, but I stayed put. There was something in his voice, desperation, fear. A raw honesty I hadn't expected.

Ponytail leaned down and picked up a black case off the floor. He opened it up to reveal a device about as big as a full-sized iPod, with wires leading off it instead of headphones. "That's why we need you to wear this." He slid it into a black case that had a wide strip of elastic that looked like it was meant to go around my waist.

I took a step back. "It's almost summer. It's not like I'm going to be wearing heavy sweaters. If one of them finds that thing on me, there's no way I'll be able to talk myself out of it."

Ponytail slapped his hand down on a box, making me jump. He turned to Richter. "Well, that's just great. If she's not going to wear a wire, how are we going to be able to tape-record anything?"

"She's a girl," Richter said calmly. "She's got a purse. We can use that."

"A purse?" I said. "No one in MED carries a purse."

"We can put it in a backpack, then," Richter said. "Something."

Ponytail made a face. "Not nearly as good, you know that. We need something on her person."

"We've got to work with what we've got," Richter told Ponytail. He turned to me. "We'll get you something no one will notice and arrange another meeting."

A weight settled on my chest. I didn't want to have any more meetings. I just wanted this to be over. But all I could do was nod.

"So, what is it they call you again?" Richter asked.

"Sky."

It was a pretty word, open and blue, made even more special by the fact that Coyote had chosen it for me.

But now it tasted like ashes in my mouth.

FOURTEEN

Three days later, I climbed the worn wooden steps of Hawk's sagging rental house in a rundown section of North Portland. As I did, I hit the record button on my watch—the little "gift" Richter had given me.

The door flew open just as I pressed the button. I gasped. Hawk stood in the doorway. He looked at me with his bug eyes and a trace of what might have been a smile. It didn't seem friendly.

"Just leave your things here," he said as I followed him inside into a hum of people laughing and talking in loud voices. There was already a pile of rain slickers, denim jackets and backpacks in the small foyer. Hawk turned into the kitchen, leaving me on my own.

I dropped my backpack and shrugged out of my jacket, glad that I didn't have to worry about anyone finding a recording device in either. After much discussion, the FBI had decided to give me the watch, with its special built-in recorder.

"Here she is!" Jack Rabbit yelled when I walked into the living room. "Sky—one of the Hummer Three!" He led scattered applause, joined by Seed and Grizz.

Blue raised an open bottle of wine. "Woo! Sky! Woo!"

Even Cedar gave me a nod, which felt like high praise.

But I only had eyes for Coyote, who was sitting on an old green upholstered chair with leaking seams. Just the sight of him made my breath catch. How many times had I longed to talk to him in the last few days? I felt so alone. There was no one I could tell the whole truth. Not even Marijean. We still walked home from school together, but we didn't talk nearly as much as we used to. We walked, and she smoked. I had been, too, until she complained about my always mooching from her. Then it went back to just her smoking.

Coyote scooted over and patted the space beside him. I picked my way between Liberty and Meadow and squeezed next to him. The length of my leg tingled where it pressed against his. Coyote rested his arm behind my shoulder, but I didn't know if that was intentional or because it was the only place to put it. I thought of the nights we had spent on stake-out, talking about school, books, music, movies. Everything except whether he wanted to kiss me as badly as I wanted to kiss him.

He had half turned to talk to Jack Rabbit, leaving me free to look at him. One corkscrew curl was wrapped around an-other, reminding me of the double helix of DNA—and of the D I had gotten on my science test last week. It was hard to concentrate when you were leading a double life.

A shrill whistle cut through the room. Cedar took his fin-gers from between his lips. "Okay, people, settle down."

"Oh, come on, Cedar, let us have our fun!" Meadow said, waving the wine bottle.

"Yeah," Liberty said. "They did it, and they got away clean.

Even the cops are saying the only evidence they've got is some white melted plastic."

"We deserve to celebrate!" Meadow took another sip of wine and wiped her mouth on the back of her hand. Her face was unguarded, her eyes squeezed by her smile. She looked so happy that I found myself grinning back, forgetting for a minute that I was only pretending.

Meadow continued, "The operation was pretty much flawless." She looked at me, and I knew she was remembering the dropped lighter but choosing not to bring it up in front of everybody. "And now the whole world is listening!" Thanks to Google, we knew that Meadow's communiqué had been picked up by media outlets around the world.

"So a few newspapers ran the story." Hawk emerged from the kitchen. At his sarcastic tone, the room went completely quiet, as it hadn't even for Cedar. "They also said that the dealer was back in business the next day. When I read that, I realized it was meaningless. It didn't change a damn thing. The only thing that has changed is that now some people are calling us terrorists."

I flinched at hearing the same word Richter and Ponytail used. To make sure that no one in the room doubted my commitment, I spoke up. "That's stupid. It wasn't an act of terrorism. It was an act of love for the environment. Owning a Hummer—*that's* an act of ecoterrorism."

"Whatever it was, Sky," Hawk retorted, "it hasn't kept people away from the Hummer dealership. It was a symbolic act, nothing more. We need to do something that makes a difference in the real world. Crap, there are probably people who want to buy a Hummer now because it makes them even more macho."

Cedar's eyes narrowed. "We did real damage, Hawk. Millions of dollars' worth. We hit the corporate machine right where it hurt, in the pocketbook. That's the only language that's spoken in this country."

"I think Hawk's right," Liberty said. "I mean, what did we really accomplish?" Meadow shot her a hurt look, but she didn't see it. "When we burn a Hummer dealership, we're not hurting the General Motors of the world. But sometimes you've got to ask yourself—what if we took out the president of General Motors? Then people would listen."

I put my elbows on my knees and leaned forward. It was happening like Richter had said it would. I made sure the watch face and the tiny microphone it concealed were pointed right at Liberty.

"You know what MED stands for, Liberty," Cedar said, "and what it doesn't. MEDics don't harm people."

Coyote nodded.

"Or animals," Blue said. "Don't be species-ist."

"But I think Liberty's right," Hawk said. "The time is coming when we are going to have to go a step further. If someone has their hands around your throat strangling you, would you politely ask them to stop? Or would you defend yourself by any means necessary?"

This was just the kind of thing Richter had been looking for. Even though it scared me, it also made me strangely excited. It had to be enough to get Matt off!

"All right," Cedar said, his face looking like it was carved

85

out of stone, "are you looking for an action that is more than a symbol, more than economic resistance? An action that is literally a matter of life and death?"

"What are you talking about?" Hawk demanded.

"Have any of you ever seen a lynx?" Cedar looked around the room, clearly not expecting a response.

Then Coyote said, "Yes."

All eyes turned to him.

"My grandfather's a big hunter. He's the kind of guy who has a coatrack made out of deer hooves." Seed moaned as Coyote continued, "Anyway, I think he's got a stuffed lynx in his basement." He took his arm from behind me and measured a space about a foot and a half high with his hands. "Like a bobcat, only with longer back legs, bigger feet and bigger ear tufts, right?"

Cedar nodded. "That's right. The last known lynx in Oregon was shot outside Corvallis thirty years ago. Who knows? It could even be the one in your grandfather's basement."

He grabbed a folder off the top of the unlit woodstove and took out a color printout of a photograph. It showed a side view of a catlike animal with thick fur and back legs that were longer than its front ones.

"Well, for those of you who haven't seen a lynx, here's one. In winter, their fur is silvery brown. In summer, it's reddish. Sometimes they have dark brown spots, especially on their legs. They weigh about twenty pounds. They're solitary and mostly nocturnal. And they're listed as a threatened species in those few states where they still manage to live."

He took a deep breath. "For thirty years, those states have not included Oregon. Now we have it on very credible information that Oregon may again be one of those states. A lynx has been sighted on land belonging to PacCoast Lumber outside Bend."

"That's great news!" Seed said. When everyone turned to her, she hesitated and said in a smaller voice, "Isn't it?"

"It's a logging company, for God's sake," Meadow said. "Not a nature preserve."

Seed sucked in her bottom lip and looked down at the floor.

"For those of you who don't know," Cedar said, "PacCoast is a small logging company that has been doing business in the Northwest for seventy years. For a logging company, they have a pretty good reputation. But they were recently bought out by a Texas-based company, Stonix, who thought their assets could be maximized through 'accelerated logging.' According to what we're hearing, that's Texan for 'clear-cutting.'"

I made a face. A clear-cut was just like it sounded, when loggers mowed down a section of forest. No shelter for birds or animals, nothing to keep the soil from running off in the next hard rain.

"Stonix is run by a man named Gary Phelps," Cedar continued, "who's known for skirting the law. He's even supposed to have ties to the Mafia. The way he works, the forest will be long gone before anyone starts looking too closely at the rules and regulations. But the lynx needs that old growth for denning and hunting."

"How do we know the lynx are there?" Coyote asked.

"One of the loggers who works for PacCoast saw it," Cedar said. "He used to live up in Canada where they do have lynx. He told some of the guys while they were out drinking at the end of the week, and word's been getting around, even though Stonix has been trying hard to keep it quiet."

Meadow leaned forward. "We could go to the media. That will force the EPA or the Forest Service to do something."

"It won't force them to do anything," Cedar said. "We can tell the Forest Service, we can tell the EPA, we can tell the media—but we don't have any proof. And without it, they'll say we're lying just to stop the development."

"Then we set traps," Coyote said.

"Traps?" Hawk echoed sarcastically. "What, we prove there are lynx there by handing them a dead one?"

Sitting so close to Coyote, I could see the muscles in his jaw clench. "That's not what I mean. You can make a special trap that catches some of the animal's fur. Once you have the DNA test done, nobody can deny the results."

"That would take weeks," Cedar said. "And we don't have weeks. The logging will force the lynx out—maybe even make it starve—long before that. So we're going up in the trees now."

CHAPTER FIFTEEN

As soon as I got off the bus, I called the number Richter had given me. A woman answered, simply repeating the phone number I had just dialed.

"This is Ellie. I need to set up a meeting with Richter. I've recorded some evidence."

"Hold, please." When the woman returned after a couple of minutes, she said, "You will be contacted at this number at eight tonight."

That evening, time crawled by. I couldn't concentrate on my homework. Some of my teachers had asked me if there was anything I wanted to talk about. I just played dumb, shook my head and said I had been really busy. That I promised to concentrate from then on.

Finally, I gave up and went into the living room to watch an old rerun of *Star Trek* with my parents.

"Damn it, Jim, I'm a doctor, not a magician," Matt said, settling down in his recliner. I saw him slip a Snickers bar out of his shirt pocket.

Laurel caught him. "I thought your doctor told you to stay away from that junk! You know what candy does to your triglycerides!" She had finally persuaded Matt to see his cardiologist, and he had come home with a long list of foods he wasn't supposed to eat. Since he was already a vegetarian, the order to cut out red meat was no problem. Candy, ice cream and chips were another story.

Matt's good mood vanished. "It's just a little treat." He curled his fingers around it as if she might try to snatch it away.

"It's a seventy-five-cent heart attack." She crossed her arms.

Talk of Matt's heart made me look at my father more closely. He looked better than he had the night we had been arrested, but he had aged in the past few weeks. His skin was still sallow and oddly loose-looking. In prison, there probably weren't candy bars or *Star Trek* reruns. Certainly not Laurel to nag him. And if I was in a foster home in a different city, how would I even get to visit him?

I got up and hugged him so hard that I could feel the bones in his shoulders. "What's that for?" he asked, looking pleased.

Before I could answer, my cell phone rang, making us both jump. I took it into the kitchen. It was Richter, although he didn't say his name. He instructed me to meet him at Gabriel Park on Saturday at noon.

"But I'm babysitting then." I occasionally sat for our next-door neighbor's child, a curly-haired three-year-old named Cinda Jane.

"We know," Richter said. "I'll meet you at the children's playground." And then there was a click.

"Rock!" Cinda Jane said. She leaned over to pick up a completely unremarkable black rock—one of hundreds along the side of the road—and pressed it into my hand.

"Rock," I agreed. "But honey, we can't stop for every rock. We're late." My goal had been to be least a half hour early to see if I could pick out anyone besides Richter watching me. Now I would be lucky if it was fifteen minutes.

The good thing about being with Cinda Jane was that she wouldn't ask questions. The bad thing was that she liked to pick up every pinecone or rock we encountered, admire it and then hand it over for safekeeping. Even though I surreptitiously dropped half of what I had been given, my pockets were still bulging with rocks. In the end, we got to the park only a few minutes before noon.

I had wondered how Richter would manage not to stand out among the parents and kids. Would he bring his own prop child? But instead, five minutes after I arrived, he appeared with a dog, a black Lab. He sat down on my bench, with my backpack between us. Cinda Jane was about fifteen feet away, clambering up a plastic play structure.

"What have you got for me?" he said as he leaned over to rub the dog's ears.

My words were barely above a whisper as I, too, leaned forward to pet the dog. "I managed to tape the latest MED meeting. Hawk said they had to fight back by any means necessary. And Liberty said that if burning the Hummer dealership didn't bring change, then maybe they should kill the president of General Motors."

Richter sat back without saying anything. I had expected him to be excited, but his expression didn't change. He pretended to watch the children as they played on the swing set. Cinda Jane was now crawling through a turquoise plastic tunnel. On other benches ringing the play area, moms—and a few dads—sat with their hands around Starbucks cups or talked on cell phones.

"And the others?" he finally said, taking a stick of gum from his pocket and unwrapping it. "Did they agree with Hawk and Liberty?"

"No," I had to admit. "There were some side conversations afterward, but they shut up when I got near. I do know what their next plan is, though. There's some land near Bend that's slated for logging. Cedar says someone saw a lynx out there. So they're going to build tree-sits. They'll spread them out to try to save as many trees as possible so the lynx has enough forest to den."

"A lynx?" Richter shook his head. "There aren't any lynx in Oregon. He just said that so that people would really be committed to staying up in the trees." He sighed. "You didn't record anything else?"

Anything else? "I've got a couple of hours recorded, but what I told you was the important part. It's what you asked for. Proof that they are considering violence."

Richter shrugged. "But by itself, it means nothing. I need actual plans, not just talk." In a slightly louder voice, he said, "Would you like a piece of gum?" Before I could answer, he pressed the pack of gum as well as something cool and smooth into my hand. Looking down, I saw it was a watch identical to the one I was wearing. In a softer voice, he added, "Give me back your first watch when you hand me back the gum. It's a start. But I still need you to get us more."

I'm never going to be free. "So everything I've done—it's not enough?" I hissed. "I'm lying to people I care about, I'm helping destroy things, I'm being chased in the middle of the night, and you want me to do *more*?"

He scratched the dog behind its ear. "Look, Ellie, I'm sorry. I know this is hard on you. But you're our only chance to get inside this group. We need proof. Something that will stand up in court. And you have to get it. That's the basis of our deal. That means you need to stick with them. If they go up in the trees, you go up in the trees."

"But I've got finals. School isn't over until next week."

"School." His stern expression eased a little. "Sometimes I forget about that. How is that going? How are your grades?"

I shrugged. "Not where they should be. I've had a lot on my mind."

If he heard the sarcasm, Richter didn't show it.

"And there's another thing . . ." I hesitated before blurting out, "I'm afraid of heights."

"Look," he said, "you have to prove you're a true believer. I'm not asking you to pretend you're not scared. But if you want to get your parents off the hook, you're going to have to bring us more. And to do that, you have to be right in the middle of them. You need to bring me back something I can act on. I want you out there as soon as school is over."

"Doggie!" Cinda Jane squealed.

She had finally spotted Richter's dog. She ran toward us, fearless. I wondered if the dog was even his. It was hard to imagine Richter having a personal life.

But with Cinda Jane, he was all smiles. "Whoa, little lady. Don't run up to a strange dog. First you have to ask me if it's okay if you pet it."

She looked at me uncertainly. I nodded. In a small voice, she said, "Okay?"

"Yes, it's okay," he said. "Then you should make a fist for him to sniff." He held out his own fist, and she did, too. Her hand was less than half the size of his. Finally, he let her pet the dog.

He must have a family, I thought, changing my mind. He's got children, a wife, a life outside the FBI.

Richter stood and showed Cinda Jane what to do if she were ever attacked by a dog. "Pretend you're a tree," he told her, and the two of them stood stiff and still, until finally Cinda Jane began to laugh and Richter did, too. The sound was oddly rusty.

When I got home, Laurel met me at the front door. "So are you done? Is it finished?"

I had managed to keep my emotions tucked in around Richter, but now tears sprang to my eyes. "No. He said he needs more."

"The good news is we think the lynx is back in Oregon," Coyote told Matt and Laurel. Coyote and I were sitting on opposite sides of the couch in our living room. Laurel and Matt were in their matching recliners, Laurel with her macramé—the hippie version of knitting—on her lap. Coyote was there to persuade my dad to let me go up into the trees with the MEDics.

"Lynx?" Laurel echoed. "I didn't know any lived in Oregon."

"They haven't for years and years. But one's been sighted in a forest near Bend that's slated for clear-cutting. And Stonix, the company that owns the land, is denying that it's there at all. If we can't get the logging stopped, it will drive the lynx right back out of Oregon."

"So what can you do to stop it?" Matt said. He took a bite of one of Laurel's millet cookies. Even from across the room, I could hear the millet seeds popping between his molars as he chewed.

"A bunch of us are going out Monday to build tree-sits. Once we're in the trees, they won't be able to cut down anything in their vicinity." Coyote spoke around his own mouthful of cookie.

"Isn't that dangerous?" Laurel asked.

"You wear a safety harness at all times," Coyote said. "It's more a matter of getting over it mentally. Once you do, you realize you're as safe as if you were in this house. And the important thing is that by doing it, we'll stop the logging."

Matt leaned forward, enthralled. "Won't Stonix try to stop you from going up?"

"Well, for one thing, we're going to do it at night. We'll bring the platforms, haul them up and get the sits built before they even know what's going on. And by the time they do, it will be too late."

"It sounds like you've done this before," Matt said. He looked livelier than I had seen him in weeks.

"Down in Eugene. Last fall." Coyote licked his finger and used it to pick up some of the tiny yellow seeds that had fallen on the legs of his jeans. "Until it got too cold. And you couldn't keep dry. Even with the tarps, the rain soaked everything. That's why it's good we're doing this now, when it's warmer. You can't imagine what it's like to live in a tree. It's like you're a bird."

He brushed his knees clean. "As soon as Ellie finishes her finals, we're hoping you'll let her come out and join us in one of the sits. She can take the Greyhound out and someone will pick her up."

"A tree-sit," Matt said with a sigh. "Damn, I wish *I* could join you guys, but I'm not eighteen anymore. . . ." He sat back, unconsciously putting his hand on his chest. Then he frowned at me. "But you don't like heights, Ellie." He turned to Coyote.

"Once, when she was little, we went to this amusement park where you climbed all these stairs to go down a huge, wavy plastic slide. She begged to go. But when we got to the top, she just froze. She was too scared to go down the slide and too scared to even climb back down the stairs. I finally had to put her on my lap and slide down, and she kicked and screamed all the way."

"*Matt,*" I said as my cheeks flushed, "I was, what, three or something?"

Coyote sat up straighter. "Don't worry. I'll take good care of her, sir."

I tried to keep my face expressionless. Nobody ever called Matt sir.

To my surprise, Matt nodded approvingly. Secretly, even though that would just make everything worse, I had hoped he might forbid it.

"Besides," Coyote continued, "these trees have stood for hundreds of years. We'll build the sit right, and Ellie will wear a safety harness at all times. There's not really any way things can go wrong."

After Coyote had left, Matt heaved a sigh. "I wish we could do this with you, too."

Laurel got up and began to pick up empty plates, her movements quick and sharp. "First of all, the climb would be too much for your heart. Second, we can't get mixed up with anything illegal. Not when the Feds are just looking for an excuse to bust us."

"What about Ellie?"

Laurel shot me a warning look. "She'll keep her nose clean. She knows not to get in any trouble."

Matt laced his fingers across his stomach. "All right, you heard Laurel. Tree-sits, yes. Sugar in the gas tanks of the logging equipment, no." Then he winked at me.

I winked back. *If only you knew.*

SEVENTEEN

Blue greeted me at the Greyhound station with a rib-squeezing hug. Instantly, I felt awake and alive. Only a few minutes earlier, I had been exhausted from the long bus ride and from the hours of studying I had put in for my finals. My grades had gotten so bad that I needed Marijean to cram with me. I prayed that all the last-minute efforts might bump my grades back up into B territory. Or at least to a C-plus.

After Blue released me, I collected my backpack from underneath the bus. It was heavy with the items Coyote had told me were essential for a tree-sitter: wool socks, pants and hat; a headlamp; T-shirts; binoculars and a sleeping bag. Wool seemed like overkill for what was shaping up to be a hot summer, but Coyote said that where we were going, it might snow no matter what the calendar said. I had also brought food—granola, chocolate, dried fruit and water. Although part of Blue's job was to help supply the sitters, I had been warned there would be times she wouldn't be able to make it in.

Blue led to me to her unlocked orange Volvo. "Do you need to pee?" she asked as I threw my backpack into trunk. "We're renting a motel room not too far from here, and I could stop by before we head out."

"Yes, please. I couldn't bring myself to go on the bus." I

wrinkled my nose. "The whole back half of the bus smelled like disinfectant."

"You'd better enjoy a flush toilet while you can." She grinned as she started the car. "From now on, it's going to be a bucket."

A bucket. I had known that, of course, but I still didn't want to think about it.

Blue drove a half mile to a cinder block motel that had been painted white about fifty years earlier. She unlocked the door to reveal a soulless, musty-smelling space with two sagging beds and weird stains on the walls. At the back lay the bathroom, as well as a tiny kitchen with a dorm-sized refrigerator and an ancient white oven. "This looks like the kind of place where people don't ask too many questions," I said.

"Which is the polite way of saying it looks like a dump." Blue gave me a crooked smile. "We're just trying to keep a low profile."

As I washed my hands, I eyed myself in the bathroom mirror. Was I ready for this? Was I ready to climb a tree and spend days hundreds of feet in the air? Then I remembered Matt's face when he had hugged me good-bye at the bus station. No matter how angry I had been, if it meant saving his life, I would do it. I would do anything.

"So how are the sits going?" I asked when I came out of the bathroom.

Blue shrugged as I followed her out to the car. "We're slowing the logging down, but I worry that it's not enough. The lynx needs more than what we're saving." As we pulled out of the motel parking lot, she said, "You're lucky, you know."

"What do you mean?"

"You were brought up already knowing what's important. Would you believe that when I joined MED, I was a cheerleader living in a sorority?"

I tried to picture her without black overalls and wearing makeup. Actually, with her cute little pigtails, Blue looked the part. I imagined her turning cartwheels, jumping up and down and clapping her hands.

"What made you change?"

"Hawk was going to school then. He was in one of my classes. We got assigned to do a project together. He talked about things I'd never heard about. It was like he opened my eyes. I saw how bad things were and how they were only getting worse."

"So you joined MED?"

She nodded. We turned off the highway, and suddenly there was nothing around us but darkness and the impression of trees lined up right to the edge of the road. I could barely see her. "It wasn't long before I was tearing up some experimental seedlings at Portland State's research lab. That was my first action." She made a sound that was a cross between a sigh and a laugh. "But I got caught. The university made me a deal. They said they would drop the charges if I dropped out. But even though I left school, I stayed with MED, because they are the only ones who are really dedicated to making a difference. Hawk and I, well, maybe we're not always on the same page about methods, but we agree that we have to do *something* to save the planet before it's too late."

I looked out at the blackness. Even though Blue had

switched to high beams, it was as dark as if we were driving through a tunnel. "Sometimes he scares me a little—he seems so intense," I said.

"It's practically a requirement for being a MEDic. Anybody who's willing to put their freedom on the line is going to be a little intense. Like, Coyote is trying to be one hundred and eighty degrees different than his family, especially his grandfather—has he told you about him?"

I nodded, feeling jealous that he had shared those stories with other girls in MED. "A little bit. What about the others? Why are they part of MED?"

"Liberty's stepfather is a vice president at US Bank—she's always trying to shock him. She's probably friends with Meadow because Meadow was a total emo when they met, which freaked out Liberty's stepdad. And then Liberty met Hawk when he was protesting outside a ski resort. That's how she and Meadow both got involved in MED. Grizz probably should have been born two hundred years ago. Then he could have been a real mountain man. Jack Rabbit goes to Reed College and smokes a lot of weed, but he wants to become an environmental lawyer. And Seed is kind of a lost soul who lives with a million stray animals. She even has a baby raccoon that she found by the side of the road."

"My parents' friends are all kind of like that," I said. "Counterculture types, that's the way they'd put it."

Blue sighed. "I just wish I had had my eyes opened sooner. I'm embarrassed when I think of how I used to live my life. I treated everything like it was disposable—clothes, cell phones, whatever. I never thought about the impact I was making. That's why you're so lucky. You don't have anything to be ashamed of."

If you only knew. I was glad it was dark, that she couldn't see the blush that made my face feel like it was on fire. "But it wasn't like *I* made the choice to grow up the way I did. It wasn't really my decision. Just like how you used to treat everything like you could throw it away—that wasn't really *your* decision, either. You were just doing what your parents taught you. We can only be responsible for the decisions *we* make."

For a long moment, the only sound was the thrum of the tires. Then Blue said, "But are you saying that you're only doing this because it's your parents' idea?"

"Of course not," I said quickly. "I can see what's happening to the Earth as well as my parents can. Maybe better, because they're more used to the fact that it's all screwed up. It's just that I didn't really start to think about it seriously until recently. And if my parents hadn't been who they were, it might have taken a lot longer." Looking for a way to end the conversation before I heard her praise my honesty again, I yawned. "I'm going to take a little nap," I said, leaning my head against the window.

Although I hadn't meant to, I really did fall asleep. I woke up forty-five minutes later with a crick in my neck. Blue was nosing the Volvo into a small clearing next to a narrow road. She pulled behind a line of trees and turned off the engine. "We'll leave the car here and hike in. It's a couple of miles."

"In the dark?"

"We're away from the city. We've got the moon and the stars. And Mother Earth will guide us." The words "Mother Earth" should have sounded silly, but they didn't.

We got out of the car. Blue put on a headlamp. I fished mine out of my pack and did the same. The small circle of light it provided was only enough to sketch in the barest outlines of what was in front of me. We shouldered our packs and headed into the forest. I followed close behind Blue, trying not to step on dead branches that cracked noisily.

At first I shivered in the chill air, but in a few minutes I had warmed up. With the help of the full moon, my eyes slowly adjusted so that I could see beyond the light from my headlamp. We were on some kind of trail. Every now and then, Blue stopped to check a compass.

"If we're going where the logging is, couldn't we just take a logging road in?" I complained after I had tripped over a stone or a root for the dozenth time.

"Sorry!" Blue said. "We don't want to take the chance of them stopping you before you even get up in the sit. Just be glad you're not hauling in the pieces of plywood to make it."

When we got to a rise, I could see stars twinkling in one part of the ridgeline. There was a gap in the velvety fullness of the forest where a swath of trees was already gone. "Is that where they are cutting?" I pointed to the space.

"Yeah. There's nothing there now but stumps." Her voice was bitter. "No way any lynx is going be able to hunt or den there." After a long moment, we both turned and started walking again.

We hiked for nearly two hours. We skirted rocks and roots, climbed over fallen trees. When Blue finally stopped, I almost ran into her.

"Here we are," she said. "That's your tree." She pointed to a tall tree about fifty feet away. A faint line of rope ran up the length of the trunk.

Waiting for me.

I craned my neck, my eyes straining to see. Way, way up in the branches, I could make out a tiny blue square that caught the light of the moon. It looked like a broken kite.

"Wait a minute," I said. "Is *that* the sit? It's so tiny."

Blue walked up to the tree and patted the trunk as if it were an animal. Next to her hand, the rope snaked up into the darkness. It was only about the width of my thumb. I couldn't even see where it ended.

"This tree has stood here for hundreds of years. We call it the Old Man." Blue stroked the trunk with her palm again and said, "Give me your hands."

Obediently, I held them out. She took a roll of white first-aid tape and began to wrap my palms and fingers. In the light of my headlamp, the tape had a ghostly glow.

"You'll thank me for doing this," Blue remarked as she finished my left hand and started in on my right. "Otherwise, your skin would get ripped to pieces. We call it tree-climber's stigmata." Finished, she stepped away from me and put the tape back in her backpack. "Okay, that should keep you from getting too banged up."

Next, Blue pulled a contraption of padded straps from her pack and handed it to me. Following her instructions, I awkwardly stepped into the harness and pulled it up around my hips. Shaped roughly like a figure eight, the harness had holes made of straps for my legs. The strap around my waist held two latching metal hooks that I knew were called carabiners, as well as a brass-colored piece ending in a long loop that Blue said was a belay device. It felt strange to have the straps between my legs, like wearing a giant diaper. But I welcomed the distraction of Blue pulling and tugging at me as she adjusted everything. It was the only thing that kept my mind off the climb I faced.

She took two black loops of rope and threaded them through the carabiners on my harness. Then she tied one loop on the bottom of the rope and another about waist high. "Okay," she said. "These are prussic slipknots. When one doesn't have weight on it, you can slide it." She demonstrated, pushing it up a couple of inches. "When you put weight on the prussic, it cinches onto the rope and holds you in place." She jerked. The loop held firm. "Basically, what you're doing is transferring your weight back and forth. With your right foot in the foot loop, you stand straight up and push the top loop up with your hands. Next you sit back in the harness, which is held in place by the top loop, and you slide the foot loop up until your right leg is straight out ahead of you. Then you pull both legs under you and stand up. It feels kind of like pumping your legs on a swing. And you start all over again."

"Lather, rinse, repeat," I said.

"And sooner or later, you're at the top." She rechecked the straps and clapped me on the back. "Okay, let's see you do it."

I stepped up into the foot loop, which was about eighteen inches above the ground. My weight stretched the rope taut. A bubble of panic welled in my throat. Could I really trust all the knots on which my life now depended? Promptly forgetting everything I had just learned, I tried to slide the top prussic up. It wouldn't budge. Then I tried to slide the bottom knot. It wouldn't move, either.

"What's wrong?" Panic arced my voice so high that it squeaked.

Blue shrugged. "You're not moving your legs enough."

I brought both my knees up higher and succeeded in moving the bottom knot up three inches. That allowed me to slide the top knot up three inches. Three inches down, one hundred seventy-four feet and nine inches to go.

"Try to enjoy the climb," Blue said. She stepped forward and stood on tiptoe to pat me on the back. "Don't worry, you'll do fine."

I felt silly, dangling only a few inches off the ground. With a herky-jerky rhythm, I began moving like an inchworm up the rope. I was close enough to the trunk that I braced my feet against it every time I moved the knots.

By the time I got twenty feet up, sweat was running down my spine. Why had I worn a long-sleeved shirt? I looked at my watch. I had been working for twenty minutes and I wasn't anywhere close yet. From the ground, Blue gave me a thumbs-up.

The weight of my pack thumped against my back with each pull. The muscles in my right leg were burning. Finally, I reached the first branches, forty or fifty feet up. Solid ground, sort of. But climbing higher was still just as much of a struggle. It was like hopping on one foot up twenty flights of stairs—and with only empty air on either side.

At about seventy-five feet up, my right forearm was so cramped it felt like my muscles had been replaced with rocks. My hands were numb. Despite the tape, the prussic cords were cutting deep notches across my knuckles. Sweat seeped into them, stinging viciously.

At one hundred feet, I made the mistake of looking down, past the trunk, past the foot-fat branches, and all the way to the ground, visible now in the first light of dawn. It took my eyes a while to find the bottom, and when I did, my breathing sped up even more.

Blue was gone. I was all alone.

Startled, I let my leg drop, so I was no longer braced against the tree. As I dangled in midair, the rope suddenly seemed as substantial as a spider's thread. I began to panic as I slowly started to revolve. My heart pounded in my ears as every muscle trembled. Was I going to pass out?

Bracing my shaking hands against the trunk, I rested my forehead against the rough bark and tried to slow my breathing. I couldn't do this. Then I saw Matt's face in my mind's eye, remembered how gray his skin had looked the night he had been arrested. I *had* to do this.

I took a shaky breath and did the only thing I could do: I continued to claw my way up the rope to the sit.

Finally, I could see the platform of the sit, although it still looked far too small to hold one person, let alone two. I heard faint sounds below me. When I snuck a look down, I saw three yelling yellow dots that I guessed must be hard-hatted workers. I couldn't make out the exact words, but it was clear they were angry. I thought of the rope dangling beneath me. Could they grab it, shake it, pull me down?

I realized there was nothing I could do about the loggers below. Nothing but climb.

I forced myself to look back up, trying not to think about the empty air beneath my feet. After letting out a deep shuddering breath, I once again heaved myself up the line. The narrowing tree trunk was beginning to be worn smooth by earlier ascents. There were fewer ridges for my feet to grab on to.

Just when I felt I couldn't go on, I heard a shout from above.

Coyote.

NINETEEN

Squinting upward, I only saw a vague shape with a beard—a beard?—and those unmistakable curls. But his words were clear. "What's the matter, Sky, are you a secret smoker or something?" And then more encouragingly, "Hey, it takes a lot of heart to climb a tree. It really does."

Finally, twenty minutes after Coyote had called down to me and nearly three hours after beginning the ascent, I pushed myself away from the tree and grabbed the edge of the platform. I was too weak to pull myself up, so Coyote's strong arms dragged my aching body onto the sit. With as much grace as a walrus flopping onto shore, I landed on my belly. Coyote immediately clipped a safety line onto the back of my harness.

"The first time I climbed, I couldn't believe people had to do this to save trees," he said sympathetically. "I couldn't even cheer you on. I didn't want to alert the loggers." He undid the two loops and pulled up the rope I had climbed, coiling it as he went. Gently, he took the backpack from my shoulders.

A grunt was the best I could manage. I didn't want to move. Lying with my face pressed against the gritty plywood, I could pretend it was a real floor, only a foot above the ground.

Finally, I pushed myself up onto my hands and knees, sickeningly aware of how close all the edges were. The platform was only about eight feet wide, made of pieces of plywood roughly hammered together in a circle so that they ringed the tree. On the other side of the trunk, three blue tarps suggested a roof and walls. If you added up all the square footage, it was no bigger than my bedroom at home. I let my gaze go out past the tree limbs, over the side, to the ground below. The fear came back, full force, as if it had never left.

"Home, sweet home." Coyote dropped to his knees beside me and grinned. Blue-green fir needles glinted in his curls. "What do you think?"

"I think it's a long way down." My voice shook as if I were freezing.

The grin melted into a look of concern. "You're really scared, aren't you? Do you want to go back down? You don't have to be here."

"I'm all right," I said, knowing that my words were unconvincing.

Coyote raised his eyebrows. "You're the boss. Here, come sit with your back against the trunk." He got to his feet, walking as easily as if he were in his own living room at home.

I flipped over onto my butt and crab-walked back to the trunk, wishing my fingernails were claws so I could dig them into the plywood. Coyote sat next to me, our shoulders and hips touching.

"You're shaking." He put his hand on my knee. "Listen to the tree. Feel it. Maybe I sound crazy, but after a day or two, this tree will be like a person to you. Did Blue tell you we call him the Old Man?"

I managed a nod.

"Close your eyes. Feel the power of the tree. Think about how this tree has stood here for hundreds of years and how deep its roots go. Start breathing from your abdomen." He took a deep, rattling breath, and I followed suit. "Just let your mind go blank."

I couldn't do that, but I found that I was a little more re-laxed. At least my breath was no longer coming in gasps. The morning sun was warm on my skin, the bark bumpy against my back.

Finally, I opened my eyes. Coyote was watching me, his face creased with concern.

"Just say the word if you change your mind and I'll help you get back down. The trick is, don't look straight over the edge, at least not until you've gotten your bearings. Be here, on this platform. Focus on the things on it. Or"—he patted the bark next to his head—"look at this trunk. Look at it closely. Pay attention to it. I was reading about this poet. He said we should look at six things a day really closely. And I realized I never really saw any *one* thing, let alone six things."

As Coyote spoke, I found myself focusing on him, specifi-cally on his eyes. The flecks of gold and brown in his light green eyes sparkled like mica.

He fell silent and looked back at me steadily. Up here, it was just the two of us—no MED, no FBI, nothing.

"I didn't even know you were going to be here," I said.

"Are you sorry?" His expression was uncertain.

"No! Of course not! There's no way I could manage to be up here by myself."

"I'm just here to show you the ropes." He waited until I smiled weakly at the pun. "Once you get the hang of it, we'll haul in some more plywood one night and build a new sit for me. That way we can spread out and protect more of the forest."

Finally, I gathered my courage to look away from Coyote. I was careful to gaze only at things in my immediate vicinity. The bark on the trunk behind him, for instance, was irregularly furrowed, dark gray, but with hints of orange in the crevices. Past the trunk, I focused on how smaller pieces of plywood had been tied to branches to make shelves. Backpacks and bags were cinched to tree limbs.

Two shelves had been lashed to branches near me, and I cautiously turned my head to look at them more closely. One held an old quilt, climbing equipment, ropes and a cell phone charging on a car battery. The other had an old coffee can filled with tools. A Nancy's yogurt container served as a vase for a bunch of wildflowers. With a pang of jealousy, I wondered who had brought Coyote the flowers.

Coyote got to his feet. I saw now that he also wore a harness with a line clipped to the back. It was fastened to a rope that ran between two thick branches. If he fell off the platform, the line would stop him after a dozen feet or so. In theory.

Moving as if he was unaware that only a slender rope stood

between him and certain death, Coyote walked a few steps over to an L-shaped shelf that served as a makeshift kitchen. On it sat a tiny camp stove, a stack of tin pots, jugs of water and lidded buckets of food.

The rest of the shelf was taken up by a few books. I turned my head to look at the titles. *The Monkey Wrench Gang; McLibel: Burger Culture on Trial; The SAS Escape, Evasion & Survival Manual* and *Baking in a Box, Cooking on a Can.*

Slowly, I began to relax against the solid trunk of the tree. Coyote carried over two tin plates. Each held a bagel, an apple and a handful of hazelnuts. "All the comforts of home. If you don't expect home to be too comfortable."

Mustering a faint smile, I bit into an apple, my mouth salivating at its tart sweetness. "Has it been hard, being up here? It seems so lonely."

He seemed surprised by my question. "For me, it's like being a kid again. I get to live in a tree fort. Besides, there's plenty to do. I read, talk to the others on my cell, document what I see. We each have a list of media outlets across the country that we call every day with updates." He looked at me more closely. "You look like you're still breathing shallowly. Concentrate on taking big, slow breaths."

I did while looking at his chin. "So you decided to grow a beard?"

He grinned and shrugged one shoulder. "This isn't exactly a practical place for a razor."

Or a shower, I thought. Getting clean up here must involve a lot of contortions with a sponge and cold water, not exactly an appealing thought. I looked down at my hands. The once-white tape was now black. "Should I take off the tape that Blue put on?"

"Let's see." Coyote reached out and caught one hand, cradling it between his own. "You've got some blistering here where she missed a spot." He pointed at a space between my fingers and palm that I now saw was red and puffy. "Can't have you getting an infection." He rummaged through the items on one of the shelves and pulled out a small brown bottle of hydrogen peroxide. He poured a capful on my hand before I had a chance to think better of it. It stung like hell, the red places bubbling white. He began to unwrap the tape.

From the forest floor all around us I heard the growl of saws. It was hard to believe these were the same woods that had seemed so still the night before. I took a chance and let my gaze focus beyond our platform.

The forest was a green, undulating sea. From this height, I could see for miles. On my right, uncut forest all the way to the horizon, a blanket of trees. On my left, it was a different story. The gap on the horizon I had spotted earlier was about a mile away. I could see machines trundling back and forth.

Coyote put a Band-Aid across my hand. "Ready to get to work?"

"Work?"

He handed me my pack, as well as a notebook and pen. "You brought a pair of binoculars, right? We keep track of how many trees are cut, what species, the size, as well as any animals and birds we see. And any time a tree goes down or you see a new animal—especially a lynx—then take a picture with this." He unzipped a camera bag that was tied to the tree and pulled out a black digital camera. It had a long telephoto lens.

"Jeez, that's nice." The camera must have been worth at least a thousand bucks.

"Yeah." Coyote looked away. "Major bribe gift from Dad for forgetting I saw him with someone other than Mom." He cleared his throat. "Anything you have trouble identifying, ask me. We'll use all the information for the basis of the reports we make to the media every afternoon."

"So far, there hasn't been anything about these sits in the paper." I felt oddly embarrassed, like it was my fault. "I looked again this morning. I mean, yesterday morning."

Coyote sighed. "They never really covered what was happening in Eugene, either. The one time they did, they made us sound like a bunch of flakes. Cedar says the mainstream media isn't interested in subverting the dominant paradigm. But we're still on a bunch of the environmental Web sites. Eventually it will start to percolate out."

After cinching my pack to a limb, he picked up his binoculars and scooted around to the other side of the sit, with the trunk between us. I got out my own binoculars. It was disorienting to look through them, so I put them down again. Even though it was illogical, looking through them made me feel like I might lose my balance and fall.

Instead, I thought about what Coyote had said about the poet's advice to observe. I looked around at what I could see without my binoculars. Insects whirred and buzzed everywhere. Blue jays flitted from branch to branch. A little creature I had never seen before skittered up a nearby trunk. Coyote said it was a tree vole. He also taught me how to tell the difference between lodgepole pine and Ponderosa pine, between hemlock and cedar. It turned out the Old Man was a Douglas fir.

Gradually, my curiosity got the better of my fear. I picked up the binoculars again and looked at the spot that was being logged.

"Logged" didn't even cover it. The forest was being mowed down. It wasn't just the lynx that wouldn't be able to live with the trees gone—it was the birds and the tree vole and the animals I couldn't even see.

Then, even at this distance, I heard one of the chain saws cut out from among the chorus of all the others. I swung my binoculars to where a tiny dot of a man walked back from a tall tree, his chain saw at his side. The tree shivered, swayed and finally crashed through all the trees between it and the ground. At last, it hit the earth with a *bwaaam-boom*. The downed tree bounced up and fell again, finally coming to rest.

"Welcome to industrial forestry in action," Coyote said drily. I had been so engrossed in watching the tree's demise that I hadn't noticed he had joined me on my side of the trunk.

"What is *that* thing?" I asked as a big yellow machine trundled over the hill and into view. It looked like a nightmare bulldozer equipped with claws and saws.

Coyote swung his own binoculars over. "Looks like it belongs to Edward Scissorhands, doesn't it? It's called a feller buncher. They can't use it on the bigger trees, but it really does a number on the secondary growth."

Through my binoculars, I watched the machine's claws reach out and grasp the two-foot-wide trunk of a fir, lacing around it like interlocking fingers. In one terrifyingly swift motion, a saw cut through the base of the trunk as easily as a hot knife through butter. The engine whined as the feller buncher began to move away from us, the tree still grasped in its claws, still upright, but now severed from the earth. Slowly, the machine maneuvered the tree to a pile of logs and released it.

All morning, I tried to make accurate notes as I watched several small trees and another mammoth one cut loose from the earth. The sun got in my eyes, and I had to squint. Each time I blinked, it became harder and harder to keep them open.

I started when Coyote took the binoculars from my lap. "You're falling asleep," he said gently.

I rubbed my eyes. "Sorry."

"I'm the one who should be sorry. I should have realized how tired you would be after having been up all night. You should take a nap."

He helped me to my feet and led me, unresisting, to the sheltered part of the sit. I wondered how long it would take to get used to the feeling of the safety line always tugging at the small of my back. He had already rolled out my sleeping bag.

I stretched out on the hard wood, only slightly softened by a pad, thinking I could never get comfortable enough here to sleep.

That was the last waking thought I had for more than three hours.

The smell of cooking woke me. I sat up, still groggy, and pushed my hair out of my eyes. It felt stiff and matted. Coyote was bent over the tiny propane stove, stir-frying vegetables. Using my fingers like a comb, I tried to straighten my hair. I must have been getting used to being in the tree-sit, because my first thought was not to wonder how high up I was, but how bad I looked.

"I made lunch," Coyote said. He carried a plate to me with broccoli, green beans and carrots in teriyaki sauce, served over brown rice studded with fat, brown cashews. We ate in silence. I wondered what Marijean would think if she could see me now, wearing dirty jeans and no makeup. She probably wouldn't recognize me. Out here, I really wasn't Ellie at all, but Sky.

Once Coyote touched my arm and pointed at a chipmunk scampering along a branch just below us. I still felt his touch long after the chipmunk was gone. Every time he said something to me, or shifted position, or even breathed, I was exquisitely aware of him.

After we finished, Coyote poured two inches of water from a gallon jug into a tub and added a few drops of soap. He washed the dishes and I dried, both of us kneeling on the hard wood, our backs to the trunk. It felt weird, like we were playing house. After we were done, Coyote simply poured the water over the edge. When he saw my raised eyebrows, he said, "The soap is biodegradable."

It was afternoon now, and even under the shelter of the tree's branches it was hot. Feeling self-conscious, I turned my back to Coyote and unbuttoned my long-sleeved T-shirt, leaving just my blue camisole top. "I like that blue, Sky," Coyote said. "It matches the color of your eyes."

Hoping my blush didn't show, I picked up the binoculars again. How was I going to do everything—everything!—with him only a few feet away at most? In the close confines of the sit, our bodies constantly brushed as we moved around each other, leaving my skin humming.

When I raised the binoculars, I saw that in the middle of the clear-cut ridge a patch of trees had been left alone. "Is that one of the sits?" I asked, pointing at a blue speck high in a tree.

Coyote nodded. "Yup. That's Jack Rabbit."

"If we're the only things standing between them and a clean sweep, Stonix must be pretty impatient to get us out. What's going to stop them from trying to force us down?"

"We're too high for them to get at us easily. They have to be careful—if one of us fell, they'd have a wrongful death lawsuit on their hands and a ton of negative publicity. Speaking of which, time to make some phone calls." Coyote disconnected the cell phone from the car battery and paged back through numbers recorded in the memory. "A voice crying in the wilderness," he said to me as he waited for someone to answer.

I didn't know where the quote came from, but after a while, I saw what he meant. To judge from the rhythm of Coyote's one-sided pleas, he was getting nothing but voice mail. Without sounding rehearsed, he repeated the sins that I saw through my binoculars. I watched as a huge fir was pulled down a hillside and loaded onto a truck that could hold only three of the mammoth logs. Despite what Coyote thought, it seemed impossible that what we were doing was really going to make a difference. While I listened to him, I used my binoculars to pick out four more sits, although one was so far away, I couldn't be sure that's what it was.

Finally, there was a break in Coyote's smooth flow. Someone must have actually answered the phone. He was silent, listening to whoever was on the other end.

"But even the Forest Service admits that some of these trees are over seven hundred years old," he finally sputtered.

I put down my binoculars and watched his face darken.

"These trees are the linchpins of an entire ecosystem. And they're going to turn them into toilet paper and two-by-fours." There was another pause, then Coyote clicked off the phone. "People can't see past the ends of their noses," he said, his voice shaking with anger.

"Maybe the problem just seems too big. Maybe people figure there's no way that what one person does can make any difference, so why bother?"

He picked up his binoculars, his green eyes glittering. "I'd rather try and fail than not try at all."

TWENTY-ONE

"Do you want some wine with dinner?" Coyote asked from the little area that served as a kitchen.

"Um, sure." A couple of times Laurel had tipped some of her wine into my water glass, but that was about it. My parents were far more careful about me drinking than smoking pot. They said alcohol had led to a lot more accidents and stupid decisions than pot ever would. But I wanted to seem grown-up and casual in front of Coyote.

"Are you sure you don't want any help cooking?" I asked.

"I'm not going to make you go out on a limb," Coyote said, and laughed when I made a face at his bad joke. "Besides, it's just a camping meal. Add boiling water, stir and let sit until it's reconstituted. You'll see why I'm suggesting the wine."

Camping meal or not, it tasted pretty good to me. I kept eyeing what was left in the pot, making sure I wasn't eating more than my share. "Was it hard calling all those people today when the only person you talked to didn't seem to really care?" I asked.

"It doesn't matter if it's hard. We still have to do it." He sighed. "If we're lucky, eventually a few people will hear about what we're doing, and they'll wonder, 'Why do these guys care so much that they're willing to live up in the trees?' And once we make them think, I think we can win."

"How did you get involved in MED, anyway?" I tried to take another sip of wine, then realized my mug was empty. I had been so focused on Coyote that I didn't even remember drinking it.

As he refilled my mug, Coyote said, "I like to ski and snowboard and hike. Cedar used to work part-time at the REI downtown. One day there weren't any other customers and we started talking about how the Earth is changing. What he had to say made a lot of sense." He drained the last of his own mug and wiped his mouth with the back of his hand. "It's like everyone can see the world's getting screwed up more and more, but no one will do anything about it. But when Cedar saw I was serious, he invited me check them out. I told you about my first action. And my first protest was outside the Federal Building. We dressed up like the species that were being killed by the logging near Eugene."

Wine tasted a lot better than I remembered. I tipped some more into my mouth and asked, "What did you go as?"

"I rented a beaver costume from the Oregon State University Store. Blue was a rare wildflower—she made it out of tissue paper. Hawk has this fantastic hawk mask. We held a mock funeral procession. Cedar got up and gave the eulogy. The cops started taking our pictures and writing down information about us. They wouldn't even let us into the Federal Building, like we weren't citizens, like we didn't have rights. Right after that, I did my first tree-sit. And I got involved in a few heavier things, like the Hummer dealership."

While he spoke, I realized I was nodding along with each word, stupidly, like one of those bobble-head dogs people put in their rear car windows. I looked down at my mug—now miraculously empty again—and resolved to act as normal as possible. My cheeks felt weirdly numb. Coyote had put his plate down, so I pulled the pot over to me and scraped up the last bit of casserole with my spoon.

Coyote ran his tongue over his teeth. "I'm going to brush my teeth. Care to join me?" The question, and the thought of Coyote's mouth, made me want to squirm. The whole day he had treated me like a friend and nothing more.

He got a toothbrush from a shelf while I retrieved mine from my backpack. I found that I could tolerate our perch if I never stood up but simply scooted from place to place.

Instead of facing a mirror, I faced him, watching him make funny faces as he brushed, wondering what my own face looked like. When we were done, Coyote stood up and spit over the side. While he walked around the sit as easily as if we were on solid ground, I also noticed how often he checked and re-checked the ropes that kept us attached to the platform and the platform attached to the tree.

I spit into a cup and crawled forward to dump it over the edge while lying flat on my belly. As I did, I noticed that day was giving way to night. Already the floor of the forest was in shadows.

Coyote cleared his throat. "You're probably pretty tired. Do you want to go to sleep?"

"Yeah, um, sure." I had never slept in the same room as a guy before, much less in a tree. My thoughts flashed back to a conversation I had with my mother a few days earlier. She had come into the living room and pressed something small and square with sharp edges into my hand.

"Here," she said. "You'll probably need these where you're going."

It was a stack of a half dozen condoms.

"Laurel!" I shrieked.

"Don't 'Laurel!' me. I see the way you look at Coyote. I know you like him, and I do, too. If anything happens between you two, you need to protect yourself."

"God, Laurel, I already took that family living and sexual health class at school. Remember—you had to sign the paperwork."

"You were lucky to have that class. They didn't tell us anything when I was in high school. Not about birth control, not about VD. That's why I couldn't get pregnant. I caught something from some guy. I didn't even feel sick, but a few years later, I found out it had messed me up inside. That's why you always have to make the guy wear a condom. Always."

I had nodded and hidden the condoms in a sock on the very bottom of my backpack. But it was clear Laurel needn't have worried. Coyote's lack of interest was killing me.

"It's so clear tonight," he said as we both moved to the side of the sit that held the sleeping bags. "Let's sleep without the tarp."

After he took it down, we both stretched out on our sleeping bags with our heads pointed toward the trunk. I lay on my back, looking up at branches above me and the stars above that. I had never known there were so many stars.

Having slept half the morning away, I now found myself wide awake. Coyote's breathing was slow and even, so I tried to get comfortable on the thin foam mat with the still-unfamiliar feeling of the bulky harness around my waist and between my legs. I resigned myself to a long night.

Then Coyote reached out and put his hand on my arm.

"Listen," he said.

I felt Coyote's touch all through my body. "What? Are the loggers sending someone up to get us?"

He pushed himself up on his elbows. "The silence. Can you believe the silence?"

He was right. The night was so empty of sound that my ears hummed. At my house, sandwiched between a major thoroughfare and I-5, there was always the faint drone of cars, even in the middle of the night. That and the ticking of the clock in the living room, the whoosh from the heater on cool nights, maybe the low murmur of the clock radio Matt liked to keep tucked under his pillow to help him sleep.

Coyote's voice interrupted my thoughts. "I was listening to this guy on NPR one time. He travels all over the world, recording the sounds of the outdoors, and he said there are only a handful of places he can go now and not hear something man-made, like a plane or a car."

"Do you like the silence?" I rolled onto my side. He did, too, so that we were facing each other. "I don't think I'm used to it yet."

"It makes me feel . . ." Coyote started, and then hesitated. ". . . I don't know, outside myself, you know, perched up here, surrounded by nothingness. It's like I don't exist anymore."

"And that's good?"

"Sometimes. Don't you ever get tired? Don't you ever get tired of trying to figure out what you should do, who you should be?"

His words pierced me. "More than you might think," I said, trying to sound nonchalant.

"Have you ever played that game Truth or Dare?" Coyote's voice was soft, intimate, although he could have shouted every word and no one else would have heard.

I recited the rhyme from middle school. "Truth, dare, double dare, fire, kiss, electric chair?"

Coyote smiled. "I think I learned it 'double-dog dare,' but yeah, that's the one."

"Yeah, I've played it. A couple of times. Once the dare was to throw a Frisbee on the lawn of our crabby neighbors." And once at a party I ended up in a closet with Jeff Appelbaum, though I didn't tell Coyote that.

"Do you want to play now?" In the soft light, I couldn't read his expression.

"Sure." It was probably a mistake, but I didn't care.

"I'll go first," Coyote said. "It's only fair. Since I suggested it."

"Okay," I said, and took a deep breath. "Truth or dare?"

"Truth," he said.

My eyes had adjusted to the lack of light, but still I couldn't read his eyes. I hoped that the plywood was so solid that he couldn't feel the fine tremble washing over me.

"Is there a girl you like in MED?"

Coyote's answer was a long time in coming. "Yes."

So there is someone else. An ache expanded in my chest. Even though I didn't know which girl it was—Liberty, Meadow, even Blue—I found myself hating them all. I couldn't tell exactly where Coyote was looking, just that he was looking away from me. *He probably knows that you like him. He knows that you like him, and he pities you for being so stupid.*

"Okay, your turn," I said, trying to keep my voice light. Like this really was a game.

"Truth or dare?"

"Dare," I said. I didn't want to tell him anything that was true. Especially not how much it had hurt me to hear his answer.

"I dare you to stand on the edge of the platform."

"All right." Anger rushed into me, anger that I had laid my heart bare with my stupid question. If he wanted to test my courage, then let him.

I stood up, pushed down my sleeping bag and without hesitation took one step, then two. There was no tug at my back, and I wasn't even sure if my harness was still connected. I couldn't see the edge, but it didn't matter.

Suddenly Coyote's hands were on my waist. He was standing right behind me. "Hey, hey, be careful," he whispered into the hair above my ear. "Are you even looking where you are going?"

"I chose dare," I said, trying to keep my voice from trembling, "not truth."

"Then sit down, because you're done with your dare. And

it's your turn again." Coyote tugged my back until we were both sitting on top of the sleeping bags. "And I'll tell you my answer. It's dare."

I told myself I didn't care if Coyote's heart belonged to someone else. Suddenly I needed him to want me, even if it was only for one night.

"I dare you to kiss me."

I heard how my voice trembled and knew he heard it, too. He didn't say anything. He gazed at me for a long time, his eyes shadowed by the darkness. Suddenly, I wished I could take back my words, stuff them back into my mouth.

Coyote reached out his hand. His cool fingers traced from the tip of my chin to underneath my ear, before loosely gathering the hair at the nape of my neck. He leaned forward. I closed my eyes and felt his lips touch mine, surprisingly warm and soft.

And then we were as quiet as the night that surrounded us.

TWENTY-THREE

Later, in the darkest hours, before we finally pulled the open sleeping bags over us, I asked Coyote, "What about the girl you said you liked in MED?"

The thought of her had never left the back of my mind, even when Coyote kissed my lips, my ear, my neck, even when his fingers ran down the length of my spine. Which girl was it? It was probably Liberty, and that thought alone drove me crazy.

Coyote let out a startled laugh. "I meant you," he said. "Didn't you know that, Ellie? When I first saw you in your parents' living room, I knew. Why do you think I sat by you at dinner?"

"But what about Liberty? She sat so close to you that night."

"Liberty's one of those people who thinks if she can't have something, no one else can, either. I told her months ago that I didn't feel like that toward her. The weird thing is, I'm pretty sure that by always rubbing up against me, she's just trying to get Hawk to notice her. Liberty always has a secondary agenda."

"Oh," I said weakly.

He pushed himself up on one elbow and kissed the tip of

my nose. "That's what I like about you," he whispered. "You're real."

You're real. His words made me shiver.

"Are you cold?" he said. "Let's see if we can warm you up."

Eventually, I must have slept, although when I jerked awake later, I didn't feel rested. A faint, watery light was already filtering through the forest. Moving slowly, I eased myself out of the shelter of Coyote's arm. We had slept with an unzipped sleeping bag over us, our two camping pads laid next to each other. My eyes never left his face as I inched away. His lips drew together, then relaxed and opened. He looked young, innocent.

Coyote's words—"You're real"—still echoed in my head. How long would I be forced to live high aboveground before someone did or said something that the FBI could take action on? At that moment, I wished they had put me in a sit with anyone else *but* Coyote—Cedar, Hawk or even Liberty. Each was intimidating, but they were most likely to give the evidence the FBI wanted. But Coyote? Even if he said something about violence, which I couldn't imagine him doing in the first place, I didn't know if I could bring myself to turn him in.

To distract myself, I picked up my binoculars and scanned the forest. I wasn't looking for anything in particular, maybe the other MEDics, or the first few loggers coming to work. But all I saw was the green of the trees and a couple of yellow, hulking pieces of equipment, silent now.

Suddenly, in a section of the forest that was still untouched, a flash of reddish-brown caught my eye. I swung my binoculars back.

What had I seen?

At first I thought it was someone's head. Then I caught a clear glimpse. Just for a moment. As soon as I saw it, it was gone, obscured by green branches.

But I knew what it was.

A lynx.

And in its mouth, caught up by its nape, it had carried a squirming lighter-colored ball of fluff. A lynx kitten.

CHAPTER

TWENTY-FOUR

"Coyote, I saw one!"

He groaned.

I repeated, "I saw one. A lynx. I saw a lynx!"

Coyote sat up and pushed the hair out of his eyes. "Really?"

"I couldn't sleep. I was looking through the binoculars when I saw one walking along a branch." The words tumbled out. Seeing the lynxes had taken me out of myself, out of the worry and speculation that had made it hard to sleep. "And it was carrying a baby in its mouth. A kit."

His eyes widened. They were so large and green that he almost looked like an animal himself. "Did you get a photo?"

"No. It was just for a second, and then it was gone."

"Show me where you saw it." He pushed himself up his knees.

I knelt down beside him and pointed as best I could. The part of the forest where I had seen the lynx and her kit was untouched, a sea of dark green. He got his own pair of binoculars and began to scan methodically, back and forth. "Are you sure it was a lynx?" he asked, never taking his eyes away.

I nodded. "I checked it out on the Internet before I came up here, and I'm sure this was one. Its back legs were longer than the front, and it had the tall tufts of hair on its ears. And it was carrying a kit by the scruff of its neck, like a cat with a kitten." Suddenly, I didn't care that this whole thing was a game, that I was only here under false pretenses to get evidence on MED. There *were* lynx in the Oregon forest, lynx where there hadn't been any for thirty years. And I had seen two of them.

"Get the camera, would you?" he asked. "If we can get a photograph, we can stop the logging today."

I handed him the camera, picked up my own binoculars and joined in the search. Coyote didn't say anything as he swept his camera lens back and forth, but every now and then he would take one hand away and absentmindedly rub my back or touch my shoulder. His fingers felt like they trailed sparks.

What was I going to do about Coyote? About us? Of course I wanted to continue what we had started last night, but in the cold light of day it seemed impossible. Doing that meant more than lying. Worse, it meant putting Coyote at risk.

A half hour later, we were interrupted by a sound like distant thunder. We turned to see a big tree bounce off the ground about a mile away. The loggers were at it again.

Coyote gave up and got to his feet. "Lynx are nocturnal, so they're probably asleep," he said as he stretched to get the kinks out of his back.

"But if they're nocturnal, what are the chances we're going to get a picture of them?" I asked.

"Now that we know the general area, I'll call Blue and get

her to set traps so we can get some physical proof. The lynx may leave its denning area to hunt, but it will have to come back. And when it does, one of the traps should attract her attention. With luck, she'll rub up against it and leave some fur behind."

"And once we have the fur, we can prove the lynx is there," I said. "And then we can shut PacCoast down."

Coyote smiled. "Exactly." He picked up the cell phone. "First, I'm going to call Cedar." When Cedar answered, the words poured out of Coyote about the lynx and the kit and the need for a trap. But it seemed that Cedar had news of his own. After listening for a while, Coyote said, "Okay," and clicked off.

"Cedar says now that we know the lynx is really here, we have to take immediate action. He wants us all at the logging site tonight at midnight. We're going to disable the machines."

"You mean firebomb them?"

Coyote shook his head. "If the wind blew a spark wrong, we could burn down the whole forest. But there are other ways—sugar or sand in the gas tanks or slashing the tires."

"But if we leave the sits and disable the machines, isn't that dangerous? They could arrest us. They could even chop down our trees while we're gone." Unconsciously, I patted the rough bark of the Old Man, then pulled my hand away. *You're not a real MEDic, remember? You're only doing this to save Matt.* Wasn't my father more important than any lynx? But the answers weren't as clear as when I had said yes to the FBI. It was getting harder and harder to keep track of who I was and why I was doing the things I did.

Coyote leaned forward and kissed me on the forehead. "Cedar says we don't have much choice. I think he's right. We're saving this one tree while watching a forest across the valley fall to the saw."

This seemed like an opening. I decided to test the waters. But I didn't press the button on my watch to record our conversation.

"Maybe Cedar wants to change tactics," I said cautiously. "When I was looking on the Internet for info on the lynx, I also found some stuff about MED. Some sites say that MED is going to turn violent because change isn't happening fast enough."

"Are you worried about that?" Coyote raised one eyebrow. "You shouldn't be. It's just people blowing off steam because they get caught up in the moment."

Relief surged through me. Maybe I *should* have recorded the conversation, just to get Coyote off the hook. "People like Hawk?"

"Hawk, Grizz. And Liberty. Maybe a couple more. But it's just talk."

"Do you know that for sure?"

Coyote sighed and looked away. "Pretty sure. It's a long way from talking to hurting someone. I can't imagine they would really spill blood."

"But what if it's not just talk? What if it's true that some-times the only way to get attention is through violence? Not to just hurt the machines, but to hurt the people who are doing the bad things?"

Even with his new beard, I saw how Coyote's jaw clenched. "If I ever thought they were serious, I would leave the group and join another one, or form my own. We have to be true to our principles."

This was it. It was time to push aside my own desires so that I could save Matt. Coyote wouldn't understand, but to get the evidence the FBI wanted, I had to make sure I was part of the group that might consider violence. Besides, the sooner Coyote separated himself from me, the better—for his sake.

"Have you ever thought," I said carefully, "that maybe they're right?"

CHAPTER

TWENTY-FIVE

The rest of the day passed very slowly. At first, Coyote tried to argue with me. Then he just fell silent. The only time he spoke was to call Blue. He told her about the lynx and asked her to set traps, but his joy at what I had seen had clearly faded. He didn't seem angry at me, exactly. It was deeper than that. It was as if whatever was between us had died. Tears filled up my head, pressing at the backs of my eyes, but I didn't let them come. I felt like I was splitting in two.

After night fell, we shouldered our packs and Coyote showed me how to rappel down, feeding the rope through the belay device. He went first, lowering himself from the sit and shouting up when he reached the ground.

Rappelling down was much faster than the slow, painful climb up. I kicked off from the trunk, the rope sliding through my fingers. There was a long stretch where my feet touched nothing at all. Yards down, my feet found the trunk and pushed me off again. I was weightless. It reminded me of the men who had walked on the moon, with their long, bounding leaps.

Coyote was waiting for me at the base of the tree. Without a word, he turned and walked away. I followed his silhouette and the bobbing light from his headlamp. We hiked for a long time in silence. Finally Coyote sighed and said, "I don't know about this. This feels different than the Hummer dealership. For one thing, this will probably mean war to Stonix. And it's not like they don't know exactly where we are. If we manage to get back into the trees, they'll have us arrested for vandalism as soon as we touch the ground again. We'll lose any points we've made as peaceful protesters."

"But what else can we do?" I asked. "The forest is being cut down. And I saw a lynx today, Coyote. A lynx and her kit, when there hasn't been one in Oregon in thirty years. If we don't do something right now to stop the logging, there will probably never be another lynx in Oregon again. Ever."

Just then we heard the sounds of someone approaching, carelessly stepping on every dead branch. We both froze. But the small circle of light bobbing toward us turned out to be Jack Rabbit. He surprised me with a hug. "You're lucky you're so far from the logging," he said. "I'm going deaf, dude. The trees scream when the loggers kill them."

"Are they gone for the night?" Coyote asked.

"I watched them all leave around six," Jack Rabbit said as we came to the muddy clearing where the machines slept. "Nobody here but us MEDics."

I felt tiny as we approached the feller buncher, two bulldozers and three hulking yellow machines I couldn't identify. Grizz leaned against a tire nearly as tall as he was. Liberty and Meadow were standing next to the feller buncher, arguing in whispers about the veganness of various food items. Liberty claimed that Heinz ketchup contained cow's blood, while Meadow countered that Guinness beer contained lard and fish scales.

142

"Really?" Seed asked in a horrified tone, and was shushed by everyone, including Liberty and Meadow. Then Seed saw me.

"Oh, my God." She rushed over to us. "Is it true? You guys saw a lynx and a kit this morning?"

Coyote looked at me directly for the first time in hours. "It was really Sky who saw it." His voice was sad, but no one else seemed to notice.

"Really?" Jack Rabbit punched me on the shoulder. "Dude, that is so awesome! Why didn't you say anything earlier?"

"Did you get, like, a photo?" Grizz asked.

I shook my head, wishing again that I had thought to grab the camera.

"That is so great," Meadow said. She gestured at the machines. "So even this hasn't driven them away?"

Just then, Blue walked into the clearing. "Do any of you know about this?" she demanded, holding out a piece of paper. "It was stapled on every telephone pole back in town."

I took the paper from her and read it in the circle of my headlamp. Coyote leaned over my shoulder, but I noticed he was careful not to touch me.

At the top of the paper was the MED logo, a series of linked figures encircling the Earth. I had always thought they looked like a chain of paper dolls, but the words underneath were anything but childish.

I hit the record button on my watch as Coyote read aloud.

BEWARE!

We are issuing fair warning.
At the urging of the Stonix Corporation, PacCoast Logging
is destroying old-growth forest that is pristine lynx habitat—
just when lynx have made their way back into the state after
an absence of thirty years. If Stonix continues down this path,
the lynx will soon vanish, not just in Oregon, but from Mother
Earth Herself. The situation is desperate. We will no longer
hesitate to pick up the gun to implement justice and provide
the needed protection for our planet that decades of legal
battles, pleading, protest and economic sabotage have
failed so drastically to achieve.

You have been warned.

So it was beginning, just as Richter had said.

TWENTY-SIX

"Who wrote this?" Coyote demanded.

"Don't you think it's pretty obvious?" Blue asked as the others crowded around. "It sounds just like Hawk."

"Is that what you think, Blue?"

At the sound of Hawk's voice, we all jumped. I wondered how long he had been watching us. Blue met his glare directly, but most of the other MED members looked at each other or the ground, anywhere but at Hawk. They were like children caught doing something naughty.

"So you're saying you *would* hurt someone?" Blue demanded, her hands on her hips. "Don't you know these loggers are only just trying to feed their families? Harming one of them isn't going to accomplish anything except to turn people against MED."

Cedar entered the clearing. "Let me see that." He took the paper from Meadow. As his eyes quickly scanned the words, they narrowed to slits.

"Hawk," he said quietly, "we have been over this. We cannot advocate violence. And if you are, you need to leave. Right now. We need pure hearts, especially at this time."

"I didn't write that!" Hawk protested. "I don't know why everyone thinks this is from me!" Even as he proclaimed his innocence, there was still a smirk on his face. "All I've ever said is that we need to keep our options open. But you know what? Maybe that MEDic is right, whoever he is. There's a lynx and a kit less than two miles from here. After thirty years, a miracle has happened, and we need to do whatever needs to be done to protect it."

"And that's why we're here tonight," Cedar said calmly. "Not to harm people, but to harm the machines. We must disable this equipment before they ruin the last, best chance the lynx have. The ones Sky saw were on the opposite side of the parcel, closest to Liberty and Meadow's sits. When we get back in the trees, you two are going to have to try to get photos. With any luck, you might even get one tomorrow morning."

"I already set the traps to try to snag some fur," Blue said. "Once we hand it to the EPA, they won't be able to deny it."

Cedar nodded. "But that may take some time. So no matter what, we still need to give this lynx some breathing room. Jack Rabbit, I want you to patrol the perimeter. The rest of you—cut hoses, slash seats and smash gauges. Pour honey or sugar or dirt or whatever you've got in the fuel tanks and radiators. But do it fast. I want us all out of here and back in our sits in the next three hours. It's more important than ever that we hold our ground."

As I took a knife from my backpack, I found myself back in the space I had been in when we firebombed the Hummer dealership. The place where it was okay to destroy, to break every rule I had spent sixteen years obeying. Around me, I heard the others laughing as we got ready to ruin thousands of dollars' worth of equipment.

The knife I had brought from the sit flashed silver in the moonlight. I clambered up the feller buncher, swung open the door and plunged the knife into the seat right at the greasy spot where the driver's head would be. I dragged it down, the vinyl only reluctantly giving way. Stuffing leaked from the gash.

Meadow was in the bulldozer next to me. She unclipped the fire extinguisher from the wall of the cab and aimed the nozzle at the dashboard. White foam billowed everyplace. Meanwhile, Coyote tried to hammer the end of a screwdriver into one of the bulldozer's huge tires. Grizz climbed into the other side of the feller buncher and crouched next to me. He had a hammer, too, and he brought it down hard on the dash, shattering it into tiny shards of plastic that pricked my face.

I jumped down from the machine. Liberty was spray painting CUT IN HELL! on the side of the feller buncher. I looked around for something I could still cut with the knife, which now had a broken tip. I had just decided to cut the wires in the engine when a shout tore through the night.

"Cops!" Jack Rabbit yelled.

TWENTY-SEVEN

"Run," Cedar yelled. "Run!"

I turned off my headlamp and sprinted with my arms out-stretched, trying not to slam headlong into something. As I scrambled past one of the bulldozers, Meadow jumped down from the cab. She landed wrong, and I heard her groan as she went sprawling. I hesitated for a second but then kept running. I had to dart around Seed, who seemed rooted to one spot. She had her hands pressed over her mouth, but it didn't muffle her screams.

A voice on a bullhorn growled, "Stop! Police! You are all under arrest for trespassing."

Still making for the shelter of the trees, I veered away from the sound. Lights from powerful flashlights sliced through the night behind me. I half turned as a dozen cops dressed in black Windbreakers ran into the clearing. Instead of eyes, they had long black telescopic lenses—night vision goggles that could see our body heat. They looked like cyborgs out of a horror movie.

Grizz ran at the cops with his hammer raised and was jumped by two of them. Another cop pulled Seed's hands be-hind her. Everyone else was running, chasing or being chased. I didn't see Coyote anywhere.

I ran faster, reaching up to switch back on my headlamp. As I did, I tripped over a root and went flying. I landed before I could get my hands out, but I was up and on my feet in a second, like a blow-up clown toy.

The next second, a hand grabbed the back of my T-shirt. "All right. You're under arrest." I tried to twist out from the cop's grasp, but he yanked both my wrists behind me and bound them together with what felt like a thin plastic tie. When I twisted my wrists, it was impossible to get free.

Mumbling the Miranda warning, the cop steered me back to where I had come from. Seed still stood in the same spot, except now that she was handcuffed there was nothing to stifle the sound she was making, half scream and half sob. Cedar, Liberty, Jack Rabbit and Blue had all been cuffed and were standing in a line with Seed. A cop stood in front of them, and when Jack Rabbit started to say something, the cop yelled, "Shut up!"

I turned in a circle, looking frantically for Coyote. Had he managed to outrun them? One cop stood with his foot on Grizz's back. His hands were cuffed behind him with another white plastic tie. Meadow sat on the ground, her face twisted with pain. A cop knelt in front of her, examining her ankle.

I groaned when another cop walked back into the clearing steering Coyote with one hand on the small of his back, the other holding a fistful of Coyote's long curls. His eyes were shadowed, his face expressionless, but I saw how tired he was, tired and sad. Then we were both shoved into line with the others, but at opposite ends. Everyone was silent, except for Seed, who still wailed and sniffled. I was beginning to hate her.

The cop who seemed to be in charge reported in on a crackling radio. One by one, we were frisked. Those who still had knives, screwdrivers or hammers had them taken away. Meanwhile, a woman cop walked around the clearing taking pictures of the damage we had done. We hadn't had the chance to do very much. Had we even bought any time for the lynx?

Jack Rabbit and Seed had ID on them. Jack Rabbit turned out to be Jack Granfeld. "This one is Angela Markham," the cop who had found Seed's driver's license said. He rattled off a date of birth that made Seed—or Angela—thirty-one, older than I had thought.

Next he stopped in front of Cedar. "You! What's your name?"

"Cedar," Cedar said.

The cop snorted. "I want your real name."

"I don't have to tell you that," Cedar said. "We don't have to tell you anything." His features looked like they had been carved out of stone.

The two men stared at each other, but it was the cop who finally looked away. He went down the line, asking the rest of us for our names, but we each followed Cedar's lead and gave only our MEDic name.

I realized that someone was missing.

Hawk had gotten clean away.

It was a long walk out of the forest, and the cops' flashlights did not make it much less dark. They had confiscated our headlamps, so I kept tripping over dead branches and stones. The cop in charge of me had put his goggles back on so he himself had no problems seeing. Every time I pitched forward, he would wait until the last second to grab my handcuffs and haul me back up. The pain from being repeatedly jerked upright ran all the way up into my neck.

We plodded along, heads down, silent, following the huge ruts that had been left by the logging equipment. Meadow, who could hardly put any weight on her ankle, was half carried by two cops.

After what seemed like a couple of hours, we reached a rough road. A gray fifteen-passenger van waited for us, as well as three official-looking green-and-white SUVs. Off to one side was a black Escalade with a small green *e* sticker on the bumper, marking it as a rental. As we were pushed toward the van, a man stepped down from it.

He couldn't have looked more out of place in the forest in the middle of the night if he had been dressed as the Easter Bunny. He wore a black suit with a white, sharply pressed shirt. About fifty, he was still slender and fit-looking, with dark, straight hair, silvered at the temples, and light-colored eyes.

"Thank you, officers. On behalf of Stonix, I'd like to express my appreciation for capturing these"—his cold gaze swept over us—"these hoodlums. These people, as they have proved tonight, are nothing but sociopathic vandals, squatting on private land, holding the forest hostage." Speech finished, he cut to the chase. "How bad was the damage?"

The head cop answered. "It's mostly cosmetic, Mr. Phelps. Thank God we got there in time to short-circuit it."

151

I stared at the well-dressed man. So this was Gary Phelps, the CEO of Stonix.

"You're killing the forest," Blue shouted at him. "Murdering trees that are hundreds of years older than this nation."

"Shut up!" The cop behind her gave her shoulder a shake.

Phelps stood in front of Blue. He was so much taller than her that she had to crane her head back to look at him. "They're only trees. They'll grow back. They just need to be managed and harvested like any other crop." He patted her on top of the head, as if Blue were a child. She jerked her head away.

"All right," the head cop said. "Take them all in for booking."

TWENTY-EIGHT

By the time we'd been booked into the local jail, it was after four in the morning. We were uncuffed one at a time and told to remove all our jewelry, belts and shoes. Our backpacks were searched, and everything—including my watch and cell phone—was cataloged and placed in plastic bags. The whole time, Seed kept up her hiccuping sobs. Other than that, there was silence. We had been warned not to talk to each other.

Next we were patted down by cops wearing white vinyl gloves. When it was my turn, a woman cop barked, "Put your hands up against the wall and spread your legs apart!" I flinched as her hands ran firmly down the outsides of my legs, up my thighs, against my crotch, over my back, under my armpits and down my breasts. I had thought Liberty had done a thorough job when she frisked me before my first MED meeting, but this was ten times worse. My eyes got hot, but I refused to cry.

From there, each of us was taken away to be "processed." I was the last female MEDic, and Coyote was the last guy. When they called his name, we locked eyes for a long moment. "See you soon, Sky," he said, his voice hopeless.

My handler pushed my shoulder. "Let's go."

As she walked me down the hall, I actually started to feel

relieved. This would all be over by morning. Even though the MEDics hadn't hurt anyone, they still had been caught red-handed damaging equipment. Surely that had to be enough for the FBI. I just hoped that Coyote wouldn't get in too much trouble.

In a holding room, I was frisked yet again and told to take off my clothes. In return, the female cop—her badge identified her as Colleen Miller—gave me an orange jumpsuit, black plastic sandals, underwear and a sports bra that had once been white but now were a grimy-looking shade of gray.

As I changed, I tried to make my body as small as possible, turning away from Miller's unwavering stare. I was shaking from lack of sleep and the come-down from all the adrenaline that had earlier coursed through me.

As I slid my feet into the too-small plastic sandals, Miller interrupted my thoughts. "I need your name, date of birth, address and phone number." She seemed keyed up with excitement at the success of the raid, bouncing up and down on her toes.

I thought about my options. I could follow Cedar's lead and just keep giving them my MEDic name. But if I told them who I really was, then my parents could get me out of here even faster. And suddenly I wanted to go home more than anything.

So I didn't lie. But I didn't offer any surprising truths, either, like the fact that I was working for the FBI. Instead, I just rattled off the information she had asked for.

Miller escorted me out of the room to get my photo and fingerprints. It was stupid, but as the camera flashed, I found myself thinking how unbelievably horrible my mug shot was going to be. I hadn't showered since I had left home, three days earlier. It seemed a lot longer.

When we were finished, Miller took me downstairs to the cells. Although it was still night, the cells were lit up from the lights in the hallway. The floors were gray cement, and the walls were made of cinder block. In the first cell, a heavyset blonde was sleeping. She had taken off her jumpsuit and was using it as a pillow. In the next cell Meadow, Liberty, Blue and Seed lay on bunks made of slabs of concrete topped with mattresses no thicker than decks of cards. Everyone but Meadow was asleep. She was curled on one of the lower bunks, her swollen ankle now bandaged and propped up on the metal sink. She watched me go by. Was it my imagination, or did she look at me suspiciously?

By the time I got in my empty cell, I was moving like an automaton. The mattress was hard and smelled like pee, but within seconds I was sound asleep.

It seemed like only a minute later that someone was yelling, "Come on, Peterson, let's go." When I opened my eyes, I saw Colleen Miller standing on the other side of the bars.

I rolled out of the bunk, feeling groggy and dirty. Miller unlocked my cell door, and I padded stiffly down the hall. We passed the cell with the other female MEDics. This time it was Blue who was awake and watching us.

"Where are you taking Sky?" Blue demanded. She looked fierce, like she wanted to tackle Miller.

"Oh, give it a break with those hippy-dippy names, why

don't you?" Miller said. "Eleanor Peterson's a minor. Different rules apply to her."

Miller took me into a little room and gave me back my clothes, cell phone, backpack and watch, making me scrawl my initials on each line of the list I had signed just a few hours before. The only thing I didn't get back was the knife I had taken from the sit. I checked the watch as I slipped it on. It hadn't been tampered with.

Even though it meant changing clothes in front of Miller again, I couldn't wait to be out of the orange jumpsuit. After I got dressed, I slid my cell phone into my pocket and buckled on my watch. "So where am I going, anyway?" I asked.

"Children's Services wants to talk to you to see if it's safe for us to release you into the custody of your parents. Otherwise you may go into foster care."

Foster care. Of course the words reminded me of Richter and his threats the night my parents were arrested. So when Miller led me into a small conference room, I wasn't entirely surprised to see Richter and Ponytail sitting there.

This was it—it was finally over.

TWENTY-NINE

"What are you doing?" I whispered as soon as the door had closed. "Somebody says the wrong thing and they'll know I'm working with you." Although I couldn't wait to leave, I wasn't ready for Coyote or Blue or even the others to learn the truth.

"Relax," Richter said. "The local cops don't know who we are. We even have ID to prove we're with Children's Services." He didn't look relaxed, though. He looked as exhausted as I felt. Ponytail seemed as fat and happy as ever. He smirked at me.

"Sit down," Richter said. "Are you okay?"

"I'm all right," I said. "But what's going to happen to me? What's going to happen to the rest of the MEDics?" I tried to keep my voice from trembling. "It's over now, right?"

"Over?" Ponytail echoed. "It's far from over."

Not over?

In shock, I sat down. I had to do something to make this be finished. But what?

Then I put my hands underneath the table for a second, where they couldn't see them. Without looking, I pressed the record button on the watch.

I put my hands back on the table and leaned forward. "But

don't you have enough proof now to keep these guys here in jail? You caught them red-handed trying to destroy that equipment. Now that they're locked up, you don't have to worry about them hurting anyone."

Richter shrugged. "The problem is that the local boys showed up before any real damage was done. It's only a misdemeanor. They'll lawyer up and claim it was youthful high spirits, no worse than graffiti. The only one we can hold for any length of time is Cedar. He's served time before for ecoterrorism. But the rest will be bailed out by their parents or sympathizers, and then they'll meet up again with Darryl Denigan—Hawk. We need you to be there when that happens, because Hawk's the one we've always been the most worried about. We think the crap is about to hit the fan."

"It's already starting," I said. "Did you see that flyer? Blue said it was on every telephone pole in town. Hawk said he didn't put it out, but it had to be a MEDic, and it sounded just like Hawk."

Doing a really bad Elvis impersonation, Ponytail said, "Thank yew, thank yew very much." He made a little mock bow.

"What?" For a minute, I felt outside of myself. Was this really happening?

Richter hesitated before saying, "Actually, Hawk was telling the truth. We created that flyer, Ellie."

"We needed to turn the heat up a little bit," Ponytail said, dropping the Elvis drawl. "Get the pot boiling."

"But isn't that, like, entrapment or something?" I said.

"The flyer only said what the MEDics are thinking." Richter looked at me with his tired blue eyes and then down at his folded hands. "You know that yourself, Ellie."

"But you're the ones who put their backs against the wall! It sounds like you *want* them to turn violent."

"Face the facts, Ellie," Richter said. "It's already in their DNA. We know they're going to do something—we just need you to alert us *before* it happens."

"But you don't get it—there really *are* lynx where Stonix is trying to log!" I was so mad I was shaking.

"There aren't any lynx anymore," Ponytail said dismissively. "Must have been a bobcat."

"No! I know what a bobcat looks like, and this was a lynx. The markings are different. It was a mom and a baby. A kit." I saw them again in my mind's eye and was filled with the same sense of awe.

"But that's not the point, Ellie," Richter said. "The point is, the group—" He was interrupted by a chirping sound. Unhooking his phone from his belt, he looked at the display. "I have to take this. Excuse me for a minute." He went out the door, leaving me alone with Ponytail.

Looking at Ponytail, plump and smug, all my uneasiness rose up full force. Nothing I did for the FBI would be enough. Unless I could think of a way out, I would be forced to do their bidding for years and years.

"I don't want to do this," I said.

"You don't have a choice." Ponytail leaned forward and said in a voice so soft it was nearly a whisper, "You know why Richter cares, Ellie? Because he knows all about how dangerous domestic terrorists can be. You ever heard about the Oklahoma City bombing in 1995?"

I remembered Richter asking the same question when we first met. "Sure."

"Okay. So you know that Timothy McVeigh parked a rental trunk with a homemade fertilizer bomb in front of the Murrah Building. There was a day care on the ground floor that a couple of agents used, so they could go downstairs and have lunch with their kids. Richter was married back then. They had a little girl. A three-year-old. They had to bury her in *pieces*, Ellie, or Sky, or whatever the hell your name is. In pieces!"

He took a deep breath and made his voice go soft again. "So don't be getting on your high horse and saying you can't help us. If we don't do something, there is going to be American blood on American soil again, spilled by other Americans."

I sat in silence for a second. Richter's daughter would have been about my age by now.

"So you can see why I said it doesn't matter what you want," Ponytail continued. "You can't get out. Not until we say so. You walk away right now and I will personally make sure that you are charged as an adult with the arson of the Hummer dealership. You'll go to prison until your hair is as gray as mine. And more than that, I'll make sure your parents grow old and die in a place just like this."

"I'll tell these cops the truth," I said. "I'll tell them the FBI planted those threatening flyers, not the MEDics. I'll tell them that you threatened me, a minor. I'll tell them you wanted me to set the fire at the Hummer dealership."

Ponytail looked at me with flat gray eyes. "Hey, have you noticed a bunch of people around when we meet with you? Do you think that's a coincidence? The only people who can say what really happened are the three of us. And who would be more likely to lie? FBI special agents? Or a sixteen-year-old girl with an admitted history of arson?"

Before I could answer, Richter came back in the room. His eyes swung back and forth between us. "Did I miss anything?"

"No," Ponytail and I said together.

Richter said, "Okay, Ellie, let's get you out of here. You've got our emergency contact phone number. And even though we can't get too close until the time is right, we always know where you are."

The back of my neck prickled. "What do you mean?"

"You've got the Ronco-brand watch." Ponytail slipped into a really annoying voice like a late-night announcer. "It slices, it dices, it makes julienne fries! But wait, there's more! It also records—*and* it keeps track of you."

I froze. Would Ponytail try to demonstrate? Could he tell I was recording this conversation?

"That watch I gave you has a GPS device in it," Richter explained. "When we saw that you were on the move last night, we figured something was up. We made an anonymous tip to the local cops, but they were a little too eager and showed up faster than we thought."

I had to distract them from the watch. "So what about that Gary Phelps guy? Did you let him know that you were going to arrest the only people who are working to save the lynx?"

"The MEDics are the reason Phelps is here, not the FBI," Ponytail said. "One of the locals here must have looped him in."

Richter glanced at the clock on the wall. "Your mother is here, Ellie. I told them it was okay to release you to her. Once that happens, though, you're going to have to make it clear that you must rejoin the others. And then we'll keep an eye on you so we can get in front of whatever they're planning, before it happens."

CHAPTER THIRTY

As soon as I saw Laurel standing in the lobby of the jail, I burst into tears. Not just little sniffly tears, either. These were ripping sobs, the kind that had so annoyed me when they came out of Seed's mouth. And then my mom and I were clutching each other under the bored stare of a desk clerk.

"Are you all right?" Laurel whispered in my ear.

"Yeah. But let's get out of here. Right now."

Once outside, I took deep breaths of fresh air. The air out here was so different—clean and already a little too hot. To the north, the clouds had sagging black bellies full of rain.

When we got to the parking lot, I saw our Volkswagen Rabbit was empty.

"So Matt decided not to come?" I tried to sound like it didn't matter.

"Let's talk about it over lunch." Laurel opened the door. Once we were both inside, she pressed her lips to my ear. "He knows."

"What?"

Laurel put her hand on my arm, then continued to whisper. "Richter called even before the jail did. He said the cops might contact me, but I couldn't bring you back to Portland. I thought Matt was asleep, but when I hung up the phone, he was standing in the doorway. He heard enough to guess some of it, and I ended up telling him the rest. He's very angry with me." She resumed her normal voice. "Hungry?"

Her expression told me what I was supposed to answer. "Yeah. I haven't eaten since yesterday." Maybe Laurel was right to be paranoid. After all, the FBI had hidden a recorder in my watch.

In silence, we drove to a diner. Since it was only eleven A.M. on a weekday, there was hardly anyone in the place. "Just seat yourself," the skinny waitress said.

Laurel made a beeline for a booth in the back. It wasn't until I was next to the bench seat that I saw someone was already there. It was my father, his back to the street, hidden by the tall booth.

I did a double take. Instead of jeans and a flannel shirt, Matt was wearing a suit and tie. I had never seen him wear a tie before in my life. His beard was trimmed close to his chin, and his hair didn't even reach his earlobes.

When I leaned down to hug him, he quickly pulled me in beside him. I started to cry again, and he patted my back and made soothing noises. It was so good to see him. Even though I had only been gone from home for three days, it seemed like years. Laurel sat down on the opposite side of the booth, alternately looking at me and the door.

"We have pretty much zero advantages, so we have to hold on tight to the few we do have," Matt said softly as he patted my hair. "And one of those is that they don't know that I know. I borrowed Frodo's car"—Frodo was the nickname of an old friend they had known since college—"and made sure no one was following me. We have to figure out how to get you out of this mess."

"I can't come home." I tried to say the words like I meant them. "I need to stay here with MED so I can get the FBI the evidence it needs. I probably made the MEDics even more determined to do something. I told them that yesterday morning I saw a lynx."

Laurel covered her mouth with her hand. Her surprise reawakened the wonder I had felt when I first saw it.

"You saw one?" Matt asked. "A real lynx? In Oregon?"

Laurel leaned forward. "Was it beautiful?"

I closed my eyes for a second, saw the mama lynx again in my mind's eye, her beauty and her absolute wildness. "It was amazing. And she was carrying a kit in her mouth."

"After thirty years . . ." Shaking her head, Laurel let her words trail off.

The waitress poured us all coffee and took our order. Laurel and I got omelets, and Matt asked for French toast. After she left, Matt said, "Why can't the FBI just keep the MEDics locked up? If they're all in jail, then they can't hurt anyone."

"The problem is, we didn't do very much damage before the cops came," I said, taking a sip of coffee. "About the worst the others can be charged with is vandalism. The FBI thought everyone but Cedar would make bail today. And Hawk got away clean."

"You're not going back to MED, no matter what the FBI thinks," Matt said decisively.

"Matt's right," Laurel said. "When we were arrested, I was so afraid I wasn't thinking straight. But when I got that call from Richter, I came to my senses. Now I'm not letting you out of my sight. We're going back to Portland, and we'll find a lawyer and fight this thing."

"It won't work." Even though I wanted to believe I could quit, I knew it wouldn't happen. "The FBI says they'll put you in prison and that they'll make sure you die before anyone listens to us."

Saying the word "die" out loud made it seem even more possible. Matt's brown eyes were snapping with anger, but his skin was all the wrong color, a pale gray with purple shadows under his eyes. After spending just a night in jail, I knew how impossible it would be for Matt.

Matt put his hand on top of mine. "It's the parents who protect the children, Ellie, not the other way around. We'll take our chances. And if we have to go to jail, so be it."

"But it won't just be you in prison. They said if I didn't do what they wanted, they would make sure I was charged as an adult for the Hummer dealership." I took a deep breath. "So I've decided I'm going to do like they said. I'm going back to MED, and I'll stick with them for just a little bit longer."

"No." Matt shook his head. "Absolutely not. We're not going to leave you alone any longer, Ellie."

His jaw was set. I knew he meant it.

"How about this?" I said. "I know where the MEDics are staying. It's a dump of a motel. Get a room there and keep watch. And if it looks like I need your help, I'll find a way to signal you."

Matt and Laurel stared at each other for a long time. Finally, Matt nodded. "All right," he said. "We'll do it. But you have to promise me that you'll bail if things get too dicey."

"I will," I said. "But the FBI will be keeping an eye on me, too. It turns out they already know where I am at all times." I tapped a finger on my watch. "They gave me this watch because it can record conversations. There's also a GPS device in it so that they can keep track of me. So if anything happens, they'll get there without my needing to call them." I didn't tell them about my recording Ponytail. It was an insurance policy, but I didn't think it was enough by itself.

As we got up to leave, I looked down at my wrist with loathing. The watch felt like a dog collar. But, I vowed to myself, this dog was going to turn around and bite.

CHAPTER THIRTY-ONE

"Sky!"

I heard my name as I walked past Blue's Volvo in the motel parking lot. Startled, I whipped around. Coyote stepped out from an alcove at the back of the motel that held two vending machines.

I dropped my backpack and ran to him. For the moment, our argument from the day before was forgotten. We just held each other for a minute, rocking back and forth, and then he kissed me. His mouth tasted like coffee and apples. I let myself kiss him without thinking, without holding anything back.

At last I pulled away and looked past him at the closed door at the end of the row. "Are the others already here?"

His fingers encircled my wrist. "Keep your voice low. Hawk has my cell, so I couldn't call you. I told them I was going to look for you, but really I just wanted to warn you off. I don't think you should go in there, Sky."

Why did Hawk have Coyote's cell? "Where else am I supposed to go?" I said.

"How about home? I heard you got released to your mom's custody. Turn around right now before the other MEDics know you're here. Get out of here, call your mom and say you want to go home."

"Some things are more important, you know that," I made myself say. "It's why you're here. MED is important. The lynx is important."

It started to rain, and the alcove provided little shelter. Lightning sliced the sky, followed almost immediately by a deafening crack of thunder.

"Come on," Coyote said. "Let's get out of the rain."

I left my backpack in the alcove, and together we ran to Blue's car. I scooted into the backseat until the armrest on the far side dug into my back. I couldn't afford to be too near him now, not when I felt so close to breaking down and leaving the craziness behind. More than anything, I wanted to take Coyote's advice. It seemed like the FBI was right, that Hawk was in charge now. And with Hawk in charge, bad things were sure to happen.

"Of course the lynx is important," Coyote said. "But the way Hawk is going about this isn't right. He's crazy, and crazy people make stupid decisions. Please, Sky, I want you to be safe. And I don't think it's safe to stay with MED."

"What do you mean, Hawk's crazy?"

"He's all freaked out and irrational. He's saying the cops and the FBI and maybe even the CIA are spying on us."

I forced myself to laugh, but it probably sounded more like I'd been punched in the gut. "Really?" I said. "Why would he think that?"

"He's convinced that there are bugs in the walls, tracing devices on our cars, that people are listening to him and watching his every move. He confiscated everyone's cell phone.

While we were in jail, he drove back to Portland and went to some weird spy equipment store. He came back with a bunch of stuff, including this wand that he's scanning everyone with to make sure they don't have microphones or something. He's not going to spell out any details about what he's got planned until he's certain everyone's fully committed—and that the walls don't have ears."

Behind my back, I started to unbuckle my watch. "That's messed up," I said slowly, trying to buy more time.

"I know. That's why you should just turn around and leave before they even know you're here. You could call your mom, or I could give you money for the bus."

"What about you?" I asked. "You should get out of here if you're so worried he's crazy."

"Because we *do* need to do something about the lynx. I want to hear what Hawk has to say. I'll stick it out if the plan makes sense, even it's risky. But you don't have to take that risk. Sky—Ellie—please don't go into that room."

"I have to, Coyote. I can't explain it to you, but I have to. After seeing the lynx, I know how important this is."

He leaned forward and kissed my forehead. I closed my eyes, and we stayed like that for a long minute.

Finally he sighed and said, "Then at least listen carefully to what everyone has to say. We need the save the lynx, but we can't sacrifice our principles—or ourselves—to do it."

Coyote opened the car door, swung his legs out. While his back was turned, I shoved the watch in between the seat cushions as far as it would go and followed him out.

CHAPTER THIRTY-TWO

Coyote knocked once on the door of the room, and it opened a crack. A blue eye peered out. Then the door opened just wide enough for us to slip through. There were seven people crowded into the long, narrow room.

"I found Sky," Coyote said.

"Hey." I tried to smile. The air was warm and stale, and there wasn't enough of it. The curtains were closed, and the ceiling light seemed to have only a forty-watt bulb.

Blue was sitting on one bed, and Coyote sat down next to her. I started to follow, but Hawk put a hand on my shoulder. He was holding a long black wand. "I need to make sure you're clean."

I held my arms up at shoulder height, as if I had been pulled aside by airport security. The wand didn't squawk about my backpack, but it let out a loud buzz as it passed my hip. I jumped, but Hawk seemed to have expected it. "I'll need your cell phone, Sky."

"Why?" Even though I didn't have a choice, I didn't want to give it up.

"All of them got handled by the cops. They're probably listening in on every call we make. So I'm dumping them."

I gave him my phone, and Hawk threw it in a pillowcase

that held a half-dozen others. Grizz, Liberty and Meadow were sitting on the other bed. "Where's Cedar?" I asked. "And Seed and Jack Rabbit?"

"Cedar had priors, so he's still in jail," Liberty said. "The other two went back to Portland. They couldn't hack it." She made a face at their cowardice.

"And I have more bad news," Hawk said. "As soon as they heard we were in jail, the loggers cut down our sits."

Around me, I heard gasps and moans as everyone registered the impact of Hawk's words. The Old Man—gone? The earth must have shaken for miles when he hit the forest floor.

"What chance does the lynx have now?" Meadow's voice broke.

Hawk straightened up. "We've come to the part of the war when the fighting is house to house, when you have to get up close and personal with your enemy. Violence has always been a last resort. But now our backs are against the wall. Are you with us? Because if you're not with us, then it's time to leave." His pop eyes stared at each of us in turn.

Coyote jumped to his feet. "Who's 'us,' Hawk? You don't speak for every MEDic. I'm not arguing about the need to save the lynx. But if we hurt someone, we're playing on their level. We can't wash our hands in blood."

Hawk's response was quiet and measured, and all the more frightening for that. "We've tried nonviolence. It's not working. If you had a gun in your hand and were given a moment with Hitler, would you try to persuade him with a petition or a protest that he was wrong? Or would you do what needed to be done?" He paced the length of the room, his hands jabbing the air, and with each step, the tension rose. "I'm not talking about striking out in anger. I'm talking about taking the next rational step."

"This isn't kill or be killed," Blue pleaded. Her tone was desperate. "This isn't our life against theirs."

"Tell that to the lynx," Grizz said. "Her life is on the line."

"This isn't what MED is about," Coyote said. "MED is about saving the planet. And we can't save the planet by slaughtering people."

"I'm not talking about slaughter." Hawk paused. "I'm talking about taking out a selected high-value target."

There was silence as everyone considered this. I saw different emotions on people's faces. Hawk and Coyote were both lit up with intensity. Meadow's face was twisted in a grimace, but I wasn't sure if it was distaste or just the pain from her ankle. Blue had her arms crossed. Grizz looked puzzled, and Liberty was nodding in agreement with Hawk. I tried to keep my face blank.

Liberty said, "Let's not be making this bigger than it needs to be." In the dim light, her dreads looked like Medusa snakes. "Hawk is talking about a surgical strike. That's all."

Meadow sat up, wincing as she moved her foot. "But MED has never been about harming animals *or* people."

"But if we don't act, the mama lynx and her kit will die," Hawk said. "In the legal system, they call it the lesser-of-evils defense. If we stand by and watch someone being murdered, are we any better than the murderer?"

He came to a stop in front of me. I had to say something. "No," I answered. Did anyone else hear how my voice shook?

Blue got to her feet. "Say exactly what you mean, Hawk," she demanded, her hands on her hips. Suddenly, she seemed taller. "Don't try to dress it up as something else. You're talking about killing people."

Hawk whirled to face her. "Is it a greater evil to kill a single human—a species that is definitely not endangered—or to let a whole species be wiped off the face of the Earth?"

"Killing someone is crossing a line, and once you do it, you can't go back," Coyote said. "You'll hurt MED and every person in it. We'll lose any bit of credibility we've built up over the years."

"Fighting one evil doesn't give you the right to create another," Blue said. "I can't be any part of this."

"Neither can I," Coyote said. He held out his hand to me. "Come on, Sky, let's go."

I dug my fingernails into my palms. "Sometimes," I said, more to myself than to Coyote, "you have to do things you don't want to. Yesterday, I saw the lynx and her kit. I think it was a sign that we have to do something."

Blue begged me. "Sky—come with us!"

"I can't." My voice cracked.

She knelt at my feet. "Don't you see? We can still stop the logging without resorting to violence. We'll check the traps I set, and once we find fur, we'll get a judge to grant a moratorium on the logging."

"Like that will work," Hawk said, waving one hand dismissively. "Go ahead, though. Be my guest. The rest of us will be making a real difference."

But Blue kept looking at me until I slowly shook my head. Her eyes filled with tears.

The room went quiet as Hawk found Blue and Coyote's cell phones and handed them back. "I'm going to get rid of the rest of these," he said, hefting the pillowcase, along with a grocery bag filled with old newspapers. "When I come back, I expect to find you both gone."

In silence, Blue and Coyote gathered up their things. As they were about ready to leave, Meadow suddenly burst out, "Blue, can you take me to the bus station?" She gestured to her injured ankle. "I'm not in any shape to do anything dangerous. And after yesterday, I know I can't do jail time."

"Go, then!" Liberty said fiercely. "It doesn't matter!" But her voice wobbled, belying her words.

As Blue helped Meadow to her feet, Coyote picked up his backpack and came back to me, his voice low so that no one else could hear. "Sky—Ellie—please come with us."

"I can't," I whispered.

He touched my cheek, and I felt it all the way to my toes. And then he walked out the door.

THIRTY-THREE

"So what are we going to do now?" Liberty asked when Hawk came back.

Hawk must have noticed that Meadow was gone, but he didn't ask about her. "We're going to do what we should have done in the first place. We're going to take out Gary Phelps."

"But will killing Gary Phelps really solve anything?" I tried to sound cold and rational, as if it didn't matter either way. "Won't someone else just step up and fill his shoes?"

"Any new CEO will think twice before they order Pac-Coast to start clear-cutting again. Stonix has a dozen other businesses. They'll look somewhere else to maximize their profits."

Now that we could all picture a real person and not a face-less enemy, Grizz seemed to hesitate. "Like, okay, can't we just firebomb PacCoast's offices at night, you know, when they're closed?"

"It's too late for that," Hawk said. "If we want them to stop logging, we have to send them a message they *can't* miss. A million people die every day. But this one time, it will mean something."

I kept a calm face. But inside I felt frantic. How could I get word to the FBI? My phone was in a Dumpster someplace, and my watch with its GPS unit was in Blue's Volvo driving down the road.

"The newspaper finally asked Gary Phelps about the lynx sighting," Hawk continued, interrupting the frantic buzz of my thoughts. "Of course, he said there aren't any lynx in the parcel and that we are liars, but he did say he was meeting with PacCoast tomorrow to make sure they continue to harvest responsibly."

Hawk's thin lips twisted. "We don't know what time the meeting is, but that doesn't matter. We'll be there first thing in the morning. And after Phelps parks in the parking garage, what we are going to do, ladies and gentleman, is plant a bomb under his car. A pipe bomb. And tonight I'm going to teach you how to make one."

Grizz looked interested, Liberty looked energized, and I tried to look as if I weren't terrified. How could I short-circuit this plan?

Hawk had us line up on the long end of the bed closest to the kitchenette. He stood on the tiny square of linoleum. At his feet was a cardboard box filled with a blender, tinfoil pie plates, two open bags of garden fertilizer and a half-empty bag of charcoal briquettes. Plumbing supplies, a drill and what looked like a half-dozen phone earpieces spilled from Wal-Mart bags next to the box.

"Welcome to Pipe Bombs One-oh-one." Hawk had a strange look on his face, almost like he was happy. "To make a pipe bomb, you pack an explosive into a closed metal pipe and then detonate it with a fuse." From one of the Wal-Mart bags, Hawk took a foot-long piece of metal pipe and two metal caps that screwed onto the ends of it. "Once you detonate that material, it doesn't have anyplace to go. So it ruptures the pipe with a huge amount of force."

"So it's, like, boom!" Grizz said.

"That's right," Hawk agreed. "Boom. And even though Wal-Mart is happy to sell every red-blooded American a gun, you can't buy explosives or even fuses there. That's why we're going to have to make them ourselves."

Making a pipe bomb turned out to be a lot of work. Grizz got assigned the manly tasks. He drilled two holes, one through a pipe cap and one into a flat piece of metal. The second hole would be used to size the fuse so that it would fit through the first hole. Grizz also hammered charcoal briquettes wrapped up in a motel towel. Liberty ran the charcoal chunks through a blender and sifted the results through a tea strainer.

Meanwhile, I became the cook. Most of the ingredients had to be baked to drive out any excess moisture. Following Hawk's directions, I preheated the oven to two hundred fifty degrees. I put white round beads of fertilizer from an open green gardening bag on a disposable foil pie pan and stuck it on the warped wire shelf of the oven.

"This oven's so old," I told Hawk. "What if the temperature gauge doesn't work right?"

He shrugged. "It's not heat we have to worry about—it's fire. If this were a gas oven, it might be a different story."

After the white beads had been cooked and cooled, they went into the blender, which Liberty had washed and dried. A few pulses of the blender's blades turned them into powder. Hawk told me to pour the powder back into the pie plate and set it aside. When he wasn't telling us what to do—and even when he was—he kept pacing.

The next step involved measuring out some of the contents of the brown gardening bag. It smelled like rotten eggs. Liberty wrinkled her nose as the stench seemed to intensify in the oven. "What if somebody complains?"

"Didn't you notice how it smelled like cat piss outside of room number three?" Hawk asked. "I'm pretty sure our neighbors are making meth. This is the kind of place where nobody notices anything."

For five or ten minutes at a time, I would be caught up in the minutiae of what we were doing. Then I would remember that all of these ordinary things—the garden supplies, the charcoal briquettes, the metal pipe that looked like the one that ran beneath the sink—they were all going to be used to kill someone. But there didn't seem to be a way to disrupt the process without Hawk noticing. And even if I did manage to change the proportions or leave some clumps in the powder, the bomb might still work. Or it might all go terribly wrong and kill us instead.

As my thoughts chased themselves, searching for a way out, Liberty said, "It's pretty sweet to think that not only will we be taking out Phelps, we'll also be taking out that monster gas guzzler Escalade he's driving."

That was it! As the others nodded in agreement, I suddenly remembered the green *e* on the back of Phelps's Escalade. The *e* meant it was a rental.

What if tomorrow there wasn't one Escalade in the parking garage, but two?

When no one was looking, I snuck a pencil stub from one of the drawers in the kitchenette and stuffed a scrap of paper in my pocket. I went to the bathroom, locked the door and scribbled a note to my parents, telling them Hawk's plan. I asked them to rent a black Cadillac Escalade and park it on the top floor of PacCoast's parking garage, as far away from any other cars as possible. It had to be black, and it had to be an Escalade, even if they had to check every car rental place within a hundred and fifty miles.

If I could get Hawk to plant a bomb under the decoy car, it would blow up, but it wouldn't hurt anyone. The FBI would have the proof they wanted, Hawk would be in jail, and my parents and I would be free. There were far too many ifs, but it was the best plan I could think of. It was also the only plan I could think of.

After I tucked the note in my jeans pocket and came out of the bathroom, I made a show of pulling a handful of change out of the other pocket. "I'm going to the vending machine," I said. "Anyone want anything?"

Hawk jerked his head around. "Liberty, why don't you go with Sky?"

"Don't you trust me?" I said innocently. My plan depended on it.

"Of course I do. But this is a dicey neighborhood. I don't want you standing out there in the dark alone."

We pooled our quarters. In the courtyard, every other room

was dark. Had my exhausted parents fallen asleep? I had to have faith that they were watching me, even if I couldn't see them.

Now I had to figure out how to hide the note under the vending machine the way Matt and I had discussed. I tried to look casual, muttering "crap" under my breath as I dropped a couple of coins. I quickly bent down to retrieve them before Liberty could help. But she was mesmerized by the rows of cookies, candy and chips. I palmed the small square of paper and slid it underneath the machine. Liberty and I each bought a bag of Twizzlers, which Liberty said were vegan.

Back in the room, we measured the prepared ingredients and carefully mixed them together with a little bit of water until they formed a black sludge. Grizz dipped a length of cotton string into the mixture. He pulled the string through the hole Hawk had had him drill in the thin piece of metal earlier, squeezing out the excess sludge from the string. Then we put the brand-new fuse on a piece of foil and baked it along with the rest of the sludge.

"Now we turn it into powder again," Hawk said. "Black powder." Liberty started to reassemble the blender.

"Damn it!" Hawk yelled. We all jumped. "Use your head for once, Liberty! If you put that in the blender and it threw the tiniest of sparks, you could cause an explosion. For this last step, we have to use a mortar and pestle."

As Hawk turned away to get the equipment, Liberty glared at his back, her eyes huge and shiny with unshed tears.

Hawk deigned to do the last step himself, using a white

ceramic pestle that nested in its own ceramic bowl. He slowly crushed the baked chunks until they were as smooth as talcum, a fine slate-gray powder.

Finally, Hawk twisted one of the caps onto the pipe. Again not trusting anyone else, he made a paper funnel and gingerly slid the powder into the pipe. "You have to be careful not to pack it," he said, as if we would all be making pipe bombs of our own in the future. "Don't even tap the bottom of the pipe to make it settle."

He delicately wiped the uncapped end of the pipe with a damp washcloth. "Don't want to blow us all up by creating too much friction when I screw on the cap." He picked up the second cap, the one with the hole in it. Earlier, he had threaded the fuse through, knotting it so that it couldn't come loose. Hardly daring to breathe, the three of us watched as he gently twisted the second cap onto the pipe.

When he finished, Hawk looked up at us and smiled.

"Ladies and gentleman, we have a bomb."

CHAPTER

THIRTY-FOUR

It was nearly three in the morning when Hawk gave us permission to sleep. Grizz began to snore immediately. Hawk himself didn't even lie down. He kept up his pacing. Liberty tried to talk to him, but it was clear he wasn't paying any attention to her. Finally she curled up on the bed next to me, with her face toward the wall.

It seemed like only a few seconds later when a ringing phone woke me. I sat up, automatically expecting Hawk to answer it, but he wasn't in the room. I groped for the battered tan telephone on the small table between the two beds.

"Hello?" I croaked.

Hawk came out of the bathroom, running a gray-white towel across his face. Outside, dawn was just breaking. Liberty pushed herself up on one elbow and swiped her dreads out of her eyes. Grizz groaned but didn't move.

It was Coyote, talking fast. "We did it, Sky! We saved the lynx!"

"What?"

"Tell everyone we found fur in the trap." Coyote's voice was jubilant.

"Fur?" I echoed.

"Lynx fur. Proof, Sky, proof! We'll be at the motel in about twenty minutes. And then we can go to the EPA. You can tell them what you saw, and we can give them the fur for testing. Now they'll have to put a stop to the logging."

"Oh, wow!" I said. "That's great." I got to my feet. "See you soon."

"Who was that?" Hawk said as I hung up the phone. He was wearing only boxers, and his chest was bare and as skinny as a young boy's.

"Coyote. He said they found lynx fur in the trap. They're coming back here so we can all go to the EPA." I suddenly realized what this meant. "We don't need to bomb Phelps. We just won!"

Liberty sat up. "We can save the lynx?"

"They got the proof we've always needed," I said. "Only this is a lot better than a photograph. We can stop the logging without bombing anyone!"

"How long until they're here?" Hawk asked as he pulled a shirt over his head.

"Coyote said about twenty minutes." My exhaustion had vanished. Just thinking about Coyote made me aware of how dirty and sticky I was. I hadn't bathed in days. "Does anyone mind if I take a quick shower?" I asked.

When nobody said anything, I dug out the last of my clean clothes and locked the bathroom door behind me. Once I was finally alone, I started to plan. I would find a way to let the FBI know about the pipe bomb we had built, maybe even while we were still at the EPA. Maybe I could claim I needed to go to the bathroom and then use a phone in an empty office. The

FBI would arrest Hawk, Liberty and Grizz. Nobody else would get in trouble. And I could tell them that it had been Hawk's idea. Maybe Liberty and Grizz wouldn't even need to serve jail time.

I only stayed in the shower for a few minutes, just long enough to rinse my hair and run a washcloth up and down my body. The towels were so thin it was basically a waste of time trying to dry myself off. I couldn't wait any longer, so I pulled my clothes on over still-damp skin. I went outside and paced the sidewalk, watching the corner where Blue and Coyote would turn to go down the hill to the motel.

And there they were. It was hard to miss Blue's orange Volvo as it rounded the corner two blocks away. I waved both my arms over my head. I saw Coyote raise his hand to wave back.

Then the car exploded.

The sound of the explosion rolled over me, so thick I staggered backward. The car lifted straight up from the ground, landed, bounced and finally came to a stop. The pavement vibrated under my feet. Black smoke rose in a pillar from the engine compartment.

Coyote!

I sprinted toward the car, or what was left of it. The Volvo sagged forward on flattened front tires. The roofline had been bent up to a sharp point, and both doors hung open. The driver's side door buckled outward.

I could hear Coyote screaming. His head was pressed back against the passenger seat, and he shook it from side to side, his teeth gritted in pain. But Blue was absolutely still, her face a mask of blood. They were both covered in pale blue-green pebbles of glass.

"Where are you hurt?" I screamed, too.

"My leg! My leg!" Coyote panted.

I leaned in the open door and tried to help him out, but when he stood up, his leg gave way. I grabbed at him, desperate to hold him upright, but his weight was too much for me. We both fell to the ground. Coyote held his right leg with hands that looked like they had been dipped in red paint. His leg was crooked, and his jeans were shredded. I saw the gleam of white bone.

I pushed myself up to my knees. So much blood! Was it all his, or was some of it Blue's? What could I do?

I stripped off my sweater, thinking maybe I could use it as a tourniquet. I looked past Coyote to Blue. She looked like a broken, bloody doll. I was only sure it was her because of her stubby ponytails.

Dead. She had to be dead. My own heart felt like it stopped beating.

I heard sirens. Someone grabbed my arm and tried to pull me to my feet.

"No!" I shouted, twisting away. Then I saw it was Hawk. Behind him were Grizz and Liberty.

"Come on!" Hawk shouted. "Gary Phelps must have had his Mafia buddies do this." He tried to pull me to my feet. "We have to leave before they get us, too."

"I have to stay with Coyote," I said, breaking free of his grasp.

"You can't help them!" Liberty screamed, tears rolling down her face. "You can't do anything for them! We're like sitting ducks here!"

An ambulance skidded around the corner, followed by a cop car. I looked back down at Coyote. His eyes rolled back in his head, and he went limp. *Please don't let him be dead. Please don't let him be dead.* I pressed my ear against his chest. Thank God! His heart was beating, fast but strong.

"Come on, Sky, let's get out of here," Grizz urged. By now,

three or four people had gathered around what was left of the Volvo.

I don't remember making the decision, but suddenly the three of us were running back to the motel room. Hawk slammed the door closed. The small room amplified our breathing. "Come on," he urged, throwing supplies back into boxes. "We have to get our things and get out of here. We could be next!"

Liberty's eyes were huge. "They warned us and warned us to stay away from the forest. And now they've killed Blue."

As Hawk lifted a box, he said, "Watch the news. I'll bet you anything they'll claim Coyote and Blue were carrying the bomb. They'll try to blame the two of them, when it's really Phelps who had them killed."

"But they're not dead," Grizz said. "Coyote is still alive."

I thought of all the blood and prayed Grizz was right.

CHAPTER

THIRTY-SIX

"I've got a possible."

Liberty's voice crackled in my earpiece, one of a set of high-tech walkie-talkies Hawk had gotten. It had a separate earpiece and a microphone I could activate by pressing a tiny button clipped on my collar. "I think he's here."

I straightened up from my spot next to the elevator in the parking garage. Thirty seconds later, the black Escalade with the green rental sticker on its bumper glided through the entrance. At the wheel was Gary Phelps, his hands at ten and two. He stared straight ahead, his face expressionless. This was the man who, according to Hawk, was responsible for the bomb that had left Blue dead and Coyote with a mangled leg.

As Phelps drove past me, I studied his handsome, empty face. Even if he hadn't set the bomb, he was the one behind the demolition of a forest, the destruction of the Old Man and what would surely be the death of the lynx and her kit.

Should I still try to follow the plan I had sketched out in my note to Matt and Laurel? Or should I let the events Hawk had already set into motion take their course? Did Phelps deserve to die?

"I see him. Over." I pushed the *Oregonian* I had been pretending to read for the last ninety minutes through the swinging metal lid of a trash bin.

Once we had arrived at PacCoast's headquarters, we had taken up our positions. Trying not to show how badly I wanted this particular assignment, I had volunteered to stand by the entrance to the parking garage in an alcove by the elevator. It was clear I hadn't been the first person to think this was a good place to hide out of sight. The corner stank of urine.

In front of the building, Liberty sat on a bench by a fountain. Her prop was a paperback novel, but she was really watching both the main doors to the building and the side street that led to the parking garage. In case Phelps entered or left through the building's back door, Grizz had bought a pack of cigarettes and blended in with the smokers there.

On the second floor of the parking garage, Hawk was in his car wiring the pipe bomb to a prepaid cell phone. The electrical charge that activated the cell phone's ringer would now also trigger the bomb.

As soon as I told the others that Phelps had entered the garage, Hawk's voice was in my ear. "Okay, Sky, see what floor he parks on. But don't let him see you. Over."

Glancing briefly out at each level, I ran up the stairs. The first two floors of the parking garage were full, so Phelps wasn't able to find a spot until the third floor. By the time I got to the third floor, he was nosing the Escalade into a space. Once he parked, he got out and headed toward the elevator.

I ran back into the stairway and up the stairs.

Earlier, I had been too afraid to leave my post, worried I

would give the game away. Now I prayed that my parents had managed to park the decoy Escalade on the top floor like I'd asked them to.

Finally, I reached the top floor. And there, parked in the corner furthest from the stairs and the elevator, sat a black Escalade. It looked identical to Phelps's rental, right down to the green *e* on the bumper. There were only two other cars on this floor, and both were parked well away from the Escalade.

Now I felt like I could breathe. Matt and Laurel had played their part. Now I just had to play mine.

I pressed my mike. "Top floor. Over."

"Roger that," Hawk said.

A few minutes later, we heard Liberty's voice. "He's entering the building. Over."

"Let's give it five, people, in case he forgot something in his car," Hawk said.

Without a watch to gauge it, it seemed like the longest five minutes of my life. My elation had already dissipated, and my thoughts chased themselves. Was Coyote still alive? Had the doctors been able to save his leg? Did he think I had abandoned him? Had Blue felt anything before she died?

Finally, Hawk said, "Is it clear, Sky?"

I moved out of the stairwell and looked around. The top floor of the parking garage was quiet. "It's good. No people, just a few cars. Over."

A few seconds later, Hawk rounded the corner of the stairwell. With his backpack, he looked like the college student he had been when Blue met him.

Once he reached me, Hawk pressed the button on his collar. "On site. Stand by. Over." For a minute, he just stood in the doorway and scanned the nearly empty floor of the parking garage.

Then he nodded, just one quick nod. Everything we had been through in the past few days seemed to have sharpened Hawk. His eyes glittered, his movements were quick, and his skin was drawn tight over the bones of his face.

"Keep watch," Hawk instructed all of us on his mike. "I'll need about five minutes."

He hurried over to the Escalade and set the backpack next to the driver's front tire. Pulling out a roll of duct tape, he pushed it up his arm like a bracelet. Hawk knelt and gingerly lifted out the pipe bomb and the cell phone it was connected to. He shimmied under the car, and I heard the zipperlike sound of tearing duct tape as Hawk stuck the bomb to the underside of the car. The plan was to follow Phelps on his way back to the airport, wait until there were no other cars nearby and then detonate the bomb with the cell phone.

I heard a whisper behind me.

"Ellie?"

THIRTY-SEVEN

Richter was about twenty feet from me, his head cocked as he tried to figure out what was happening. Then he saw Hawk's feet as he started to wiggle out from underneath the Escalade. Richter quickly drew his gun and went into a crouch.

I dashed forward and grabbed the backpack, pulling it out of Hawk's reach in case he decided to blow us all up when he realized it was over. But as I did, I heard an enormous grunt and a clunk. Grizz stood over the crumpled body of Richter. In his hands, he clutched the metal top of a trash can.

Panting heavily, Grizz said, "Like, I saw this guy drive up real fast, and then he parked on the sidewalk and took off running. I figured it had to be about what we were doing, so I ran after him. When I got to the top of the stairs, I saw him pull his gun on you."

I hardly heard Grizz's words. I couldn't take my eyes off Richter. He was sprawled facedown, his head turned to one side. Blood trickled out of his left ear, bright red against skin that suddenly looked so white.

Hawk was now out from under the car, his eyes darting back and forth between me and Richter's unmoving form. Before I could react, he jerked the backpack out of my hands and grabbed my elbow.

"Give me his gun," he ordered Grizz. He slung the back-pack over his shoulder.

Grizz picked up the gun from where it lay next to Richter's slack hand. Holding it pinched between thumb and forefinger, he handed it to Hawk. Hawk took the gun and held it like he meant it. He still had a tight grip on my arm.

"Now get out his wallet and see who he is. And be ready to hit him again if he moves." As he spoke, Hawk whipped his head from side to side, making sure we were still alone.

Grizz pulled the wallet from Richter's back pocket and flipped it open. He stared at the gold shield. "His name's John Richter. Dude—he's with the FBI."

Hawk said, "I heard him say your name, Sky. Or should I say Ellie? Why does an FBI agent know your real name?"

I opened my mouth, but no words came out. Desperately, I tried to think of an answer. But as Hawk's expression hard-ened, I realized my pause had been an answer all by itself.

He jabbed the gun into my belly and said to Grizz, "There's a roll of duct tape under the car. Tape his mouth and his hands together behind his back and his ankles too. Then shove him under the car far enough that no one will see him. And do it fast before someone comes up here."

"Man, wait a minute," Grizz said. "Why *did* he know Sky?"

"Because she sold us out," Hawk said grimly.

"She what?" Grizz's mouth dropped open. A pink piece of gum lay on his tongue.

"We don't have time to discuss this," Hawk hissed. The gun

wasn't pointing in Grizz's direction, but it wasn't exactly pointing away, either.

Grizz set down the top of the trash can and began to drag Richter by his ankles. I winced as his head bounced along the pavement. When I opened my mouth to ask Grizz to be careful, Hawk jammed the gun in my belly harder.

"Don't make a sound or I'll shoot you right now." Hawk pulled me back behind a retaining wall so that we were out of sight of the elevator and the stairwell.

Grizz finished taping Richter's ankles. "Should I hog-tie him?" he asked, looking up at Hawk. "You know, tie his ankles to his hands?"

"I know what hog-tie means!" Hawk snapped. "We don't have time for that. Just push him far enough underneath the car that Phelps won't see him."

"But, man, what about the bomb?" Grizz wrinkled his forehead. "It's under there."

"I've got that thing duct-taped on good. We'll do it as soon as Phelps gets back in the car. It will be a two-fer."

"But this guy is with the FBI, not Stonix!" Grizz looked confused. "What does he have to do with what's happening to the forest?"

"He was trying to stop us, can't you see that? Sometimes there are unintentional casualties. Sometimes we just do what we have to do. And we *have* to do this. Now, come on, we need to get out of here." Hawk shook me. "Who else knows? Does Phelps know?"

"I don't know," I answered honestly. "I don't think so."

"You'd better hope that he doesn't."

There was a crackle in my ear. I watched the others stiffen as we all listened to Liberty's voice on our earpieces. "He's leaving. Over."

Hawk twisted his head to push his microphone button with his chin. "Liberty, we've got a situation. Change of plans. Follow Phelps. Stay close and pretend you're just going to another car on the same floor. And let me know the second he gets inside his car. Over."

In my ear, Liberty's voice sounded more high-pitched than usual. "Why? What happened?"

"Just do what I say and don't ask questions!"

"Okay." Her voice wavered. "Over."

"We've got to get out of here," Hawk said to Grizz. "Now. I don't want Sky warning Phelps away."

We marched over to the stairway. Hawk pushed me forward, and I stumbled down two stairs before I caught myself. Hawk had pulled his cell phone from his backpack, so he now held the gun in one hand and the cell phone in the other.

"Please," I begged. "It's not right. If we kill an FBI agent, they won't rest until they've hunted us down."

"Don't use the word 'us,' traitor." Hawk gave me another vicious shove. "We're going back to my car. And if you make a sound, I swear to God, I'll kill you."

One step behind Hawk, Grizz looked scared and confused. His eyes kept darting between Hawk and me. Clearly, he didn't know what to do.

As the three of us walked out into the second floor of the

parking garage, I prayed there would be something there, a witness, a distraction, maybe even a passerby who could help me. But there was no one.

When we reached the car, Hawk said, "Get in the back and scoot over." I climbed in, stepping over the open toolbox on the floor behind the front passenger seat. As I did, Hawk took the keys from his pocket and handed them to Grizz. "You're driving. Let's go."

The big man balked. "What about Liberty?"

"We'll wait for her outside," Hawk said impatiently. "Now come on, we've got to go."

Grizz went around the car and got in the front seat while Hawk got in the backseat with me. He slammed his door closed and leaned forward. "Come on! I'd like to be out of here before the bomb blows up." With his chin, he pressed his microphone. "Liberty, is he in the car yet? Over."

We all heard Liberty's voice. "I thought we were going to wait until he was by himself on the freeway. Because there's a car parked next to his and little kids are getting out of it. There are kids!"

"So he's in the vehicle, then?"

"You can't, Hawk!" Liberty shouted, her voice breaking.

Hawk looked past me, seeming to focus on the distance. "Collateral damage," he said quietly.

No! Richter will die!

I lunged for his phone, clawing his arm, but he held the phone out of my grasp. I reached higher, the skin of his cheek gathering under my fingernails as I drew blood. Hawk wedged his knee into my stomach, knocking the air out of me. I couldn't breathe, but I couldn't let that stop me. I turned my head and closed my teeth on his arm. My mouth filled with the copper taste of blood.

And Hawk's arm dropped just enough. I felt a surge of triumph as my fingers finally closed on the phone.

Bang! The gun went off. It felt like someone had punched me in the arm. Then pain seared through me, so big it wasn't even pain, but something more.

From above us came an echoing boom that obliterated all other sounds.

All I could think was that I still seemed to be alive. And Richter wasn't.

THIRTY-EIGHT

Slowly, I turned my head and looked down at my side. Bright red blood covered my left arm and torso. As I watched it drip off my fingers, I realized it was mine. Somewhere above us, a woman screamed and screamed, her voice ragged with hysteria.

Grizz fumbled with the microphone on his collar. "Liberty, come in, over? Liberty?"

The only answer was the crackle of static.

"Drive!" Hawk demanded. He poked the gun against the back of Grizz's neck. "We have to get out of here!"

"Are you going to shoot me, too?" Grizz shouted. He threw open the car door and ran toward the exit. Hawk cursed and jammed his skinny legs between the two bucket seats, wiggling into the driver's seat. With a grind, he started the engine and jammed it into reverse.

"Stop! FBI!" The shout echoed off the walls.

I jerked my head around to see Ponytail crouched about twenty feet away, holding his gun with both hands.

Rather than stopping, Hawk spun the wheel until the car was aimed directly at the FBI agent. So was the gun Hawk had taken from Richter.

I threw myself down in the seat. The seat belt buckle dug into my shoulder like a red-hot poker. I heard two shots in quick succession and the sound of shattering glass. Sharp flecks peppered my cheeks, my ear, my hair.

The car lurched to a stop, shuddered and died.

"Put down your weapon and get out of the car with your hands up!"

The voice was familiar, but it didn't belong to Ponytail. I risked peeking over the seat through the shattered windshield.

It was Matt. He was holding Ponytail's gun, but with a lot less authority than an FBI agent. Ponytail writhed on the ground, pressing both hands hard against his right thigh. Blood had already darkened his pant leg.

Hawk must have shot Ponytail through the windshield. And judging by the steam rising from the hood, Ponytail had shot the engine.

Hawk slowly raised his left hand. His right, however, paid no attention to my father's command. Instead, it rested the gun on the dash. Pointed straight at Matt's chest.

He was going to shoot my father!

I scrabbled in the tool chest, grabbing the screwdriver Hawk had used to finish the pipe bomb. Ignoring the waves of pain from my injured arm, I leaned forward and pressed the point against his neck.

"Drop the gun!" I yelled.

Hawk didn't move.

I pressed harder, watching his skin dimple. A drop of blood oozed out. I could almost see the blood running like a column just underneath his skin. Part of me wanted to push the screwdriver until the skin yielded with a pop.

"Drop it!" I yelled again.

But still Hawk hesitated. The blood ran faster now, trickling down his neck. Another drop landed on his thigh. With a curse, he finally released the gun.

I snatched it up from the passenger seat, yanked open the back door and scrambled out. Heedless of the pain in my arm, I wrapped my left hand around my right fist, holding the gun out in front of me, my legs apart and knees slightly bent, the way I had seen Ponytail stand. Matt and I were shoulder-to-shoulder, both our guns pointing at Hawk.

"Don't move, Hawk, or I'll shoot," I said.

"That's right, she will," said a man behind me.

It was Richter. He was uninjured, except for the drying blood below his ear. Pieces of duct tape dangled from the bottom of his pants legs. He took the gun from my hands.

Wearing a funny expression, Matt abruptly sat down on the ground next to Ponytail. "Ellie?" he started. "I think—"

But I never got to hear what he thought. My father slumped over, and his head made a horrible hollow sound as it hit the ground.

Coyote's leg, encased in a white cast from heel to hip, hung suspended above the hospital bed. Tubes led from an IV stand to the back of his hand. The left side of his face was purpled with bruises.

I sat in the chair beside his bed. Even asleep, Coyote's expression was uneasy. His eyes moved back and forth under closed lids.

Finally, they opened. He blinked several times, struggling to focus. After a long moment, Coyote seemed to take in who I was. His eyes widened and the right corner of his mouth turned up. When he noticed my sling and bandaged shoulder, his expression turned to concern.

"You're hurt!" Wincing, he pushed himself up on his elbows.

"It's not too bad," I said. "Just a scrape."

"What about Hawk and the rest? Did they hurt anyone?"

"They tried, but they got stopped in time. Hawk's in jail. So are Grizz and Liberty, although the charges they're facing aren't as serious."

His face hardened. "Blue's dead," he said bluntly. "You might not know that since you ran off."

Tears wetted the corners of my eyes, but I blinked them back. "I know she's dead."

"You know who told me? The cops. I wake up six hours after the accident, tubes coming out of everyplace, my leg in traction, and they tell me she's dead. The bomb must have been right under her seat. And then they tell me I'm under arrest for possession of explosives. They said we did it to ourselves, that we were transporting a bomb!"

"What did you do?"

"I guess my survival instinct kicked in, despite everything else. I said, 'I won't talk to you without a lawyer.' And then I passed out." He tilted his head. "But now everything seems to have changed, except I don't know why. I haven't seen a lawyer yet, but I haven't seen a cop, either."

"That's because they know now that it was Hawk who set the bomb under your car, not you guys."

"Hawk?" I saw Coyote's eyes widen as he struggled with the truth. "But why would he bomb us? We're MEDics, too!"

"He turned against you when you wouldn't go along with his plans. He had already made a bomb while the rest of us were in jail. While you guys were packing up, he went outside to get rid of the phones and put that bomb under Blue's car. Then he had us make another one for Phelps. Hawk thought he could blame your deaths on Phelps's Mafia connections and turn you into martyrs for the cause. You were right. He wasn't really thinking straight."

"I knew Hawk was crazy," Coyote said. "That's why I told you to leave."

I took a deep breath and forced the words out before I lost my courage. "There's something else I need to tell you. There was a reason I stayed with Hawk. I was working undercover with the FBI."

I waited anxiously for his reaction, unable to read his expression. Finally, Coyote gave me a half smile that didn't quite reach his eyes. "You're joking, right? The FBI? The guys in dark suits and dark glasses?"

"I'm serious. But Coyote, I swear it wasn't my idea. While the FBI was watching you guys, they found out my parents were growing pot and arrested them. They said if I joined MED and told them what you guys were doing, then my parents wouldn't have to go to jail and I wouldn't have to go into foster care."

"You were spying on us?" he said slowly.

"Yes. It wasn't my choice, but yes. It was either that, or they said Matt would die in jail."

Coyote narrowed his eyes. "So—you never believed in MED?"

"I don't know," I said. "I do care about what's happening to the Earth, even though I had never thought about how to stop it. But when I saw that lynx . . ." I took a deep breath. "The only reason I stayed with Hawk was so that I could stop them from hurting anyone."

"Did you stop them?" He looked at my bandaged arm. "And how did you get hurt?"

"Hawk was going to blow up Phelps's car. But I got Matt and Laurel to rent the same kind of car and park it in the garage, and I tricked Hawk into putting the bomb there." I told Coyote how Richter had ended up under the decoy car and how Hawk shot me before Matt showed up. "But after every-thing that happened, my dad had a heart attack. The doctors say he should be okay, since they got him to the hospital right away. In fact, he's on the floor above you, with Laurel glued to his side."

Talking about it, I still felt shaky. I had come so close to losing everyone I cared about. And in Blue's case, we had all lost. I choked out, "I still can't believe Blue is gone."

Coyote's voice was cold. "Did you ever think maybe she wouldn't be dead if you hadn't gotten involved?"

"What? What are you talking about?"

"If you hadn't joined MED under false pretenses, you wouldn't have seen the lynx. Then Hawk wouldn't have been so desperate to stop the logging that he was willing to kill in-nocent people." His eyes glittered like green glass. "Or did you even *see* the lynx? Did you lie about that, too?"

"Of course I saw the lynx!"

"And what about you and me?" The muscles in Coyote's jaw were clenched so tight he had to force the words out. "Did they order you to do that, too?"

"No! What happened between you and me was real. I—I love you, Coyote."

My words hung in the air. Coyote opened his mouth, but didn't speak. Finally he whispered, "You love me." It didn't sound like a question or a challenge, but a statement of fact.

I nodded.

His voice got stronger. "But you don't even know me." The anger returned to his eyes. "And I don't think I know you."

"But I think we *do* know the important stuff. At least we do now." I got up to leave. "Look, I don't expect you to feel the same way. And I don't expect you to do anything about it. I just wanted you to know."

I had my hand on the doorknob when Coyote said, "Wait."

FORTY

Coyote's expression was unreadable. "You never told me what happened in the forest. Are they still logging?"

If all he wanted was facts, I could give him facts. "Gary Phelps has already made an announcement to the press. I'm not sure if it's because he was frightened off by the bombs or because they recovered the traps with the lynx's fur from the trunk of Blue's car. But at least she didn't die for nothing. Stonix has stopped the logging."

As I talked, I realized I wasn't sad anymore. I was angry. "Maybe you're right," I continued. "Maybe if I had just kept out of this, Gary Phelps and maybe a bunch of other people besides Blue would have been dead. Can't you see I did the best I could? I just didn't want anybody to die!"

There was a long silence. I looked up from the toes of my clogs and into Coyote's bright green eyes.

He let out a long, shuddering sigh. "I'm sorry. Maybe I was too hard on you. I knew something was going on, but I never guessed it was that. And then when I thought that you had been doing everything on someone else's orders, that it meant nothing, well, I . . . I guess I went off the deep end."

"I'm still me, Coyote." I dashed the tears from my eyes. "I'm still me."

"You're right," Coyote said. "About what you said earlier. Maybe we do know the really important stuff about each other. . . . Why don't you give me a kiss?"

"What?" I knew I had gotten through to him, but this seemed too fast.

He nodded emphatically. "Give me a kiss, Ellie."

I took three steps toward his bed and leaned over, bracing my good hand on the wall. He put his hand on my neck and pulled me closer, turning my head so that his lips rested against my ear. "So are we being recorded now? Is this room bugged?"

I shrugged. Who was to know when it came to the FBI?

He whispered, "The fur was from the lynx in my grandfather's basement."

I pulled back and looked at him. He tugged me close again. "Come on. We both know the lynx is there. I just bought it some time. When the bomb under our car went off, we weren't coming back from the forest—we were coming back from Portland. We put the fur in an extra trap, and we were going to say it came from the parcel." Still in a whisper, Coyote added, "There's something else. The cops gave me back my watch. They found it in the car. Only it wasn't mine."

My hand went unconsciously to my wrist.

"I *had* seen the watch before, but I didn't tell them that. You used to wear it. And last night, when I couldn't sleep, I played around with it a little. It has some pretty interesting features."

Now I understood why he had been so quick to believe me

about the FBI. And that he'd had hours to get angry. "You didn't erase anything, did you?"

"I thought about it at first, but then I decided not to. Not until I heard what you had to say about everything."

My knees went weak in relief. "Thank God! Where is it?"

He pointed with his chin. "In my bedside drawer."

I took the watch out and strapped it on. When they had first given it to me, I had hated it. Now it felt like my armor.

Coyote's eyes were blinking more and more slowly, like a little kid fighting sleep. "Sorry," he said in a normal voice. He gave me a lopsided smile that nearly broke my heart. "They keep me pretty doped up."

"I'll let you get some rest, then."

"Just one more kiss," he said, even though he hadn't kissed me the first time. I figured he was still speaking as if someone else was listening.

He hooked a finger under my chin and this time he really did bring my lips down to meet his. His mouth was soft and full. I kissed him gently, mindful of the purple bruises on his face.

A minute or an hour later I lifted my head.

"I'd better go." When I straightened up, my head felt like it could pop off and float away. Coyote's eyes were already closed.

Slowly, I backed out the door, eased it closed against the noise in the hall. On tiptoe, I turned away.

I stifled a gasp when I saw who was standing right behind me.

Ponytail was leaning on a cane. His navy blue sweatpants were as tight as a sausage skin over his bandaged right thigh. His skin was gray, and his eyes were shadowed. He looked ten years older than when I had seen him last.

"I need a word with you." He laid his free hand on my arm.

I shook him off. "I don't think so. I'm not interested in talking to you." I didn't bother to hide how much he pissed me off. It was all over, and I didn't need to do what Ponytail said anymore.

"We're going to need you to testify against Hawk and the others."

I took a step back. "You already have all the proof you need without me. I want this to be over."

Ponytail sneered. "It doesn't matter what you want. We need to be able to lock up Darryl Denigan and throw away the key. And that means having you testify about building and placing the pipe bomb, about him shooting me, about all of it."

"No. I want my normal life back. I want to forget we ever met."

Ponytail gave his head an exaggerated shake. "Well, then, you'll be in very big trouble, Ellie. We can charge you with arson, conspiracy and aiding and abetting. And your parents can be charged with maintaining a dwelling for the purpose of—"

I cut him off. "Come on, you already have eyewitness testimony, yours and Richter's. I did what you wanted me to do, and now I'm done, and you're not going to charge me or my parents with anything. And, for that matter, you're not going to charge Coyote, either."

Ponytail grimaced as he shifted his weight to his good leg. "You want to tell me why I shouldn't arrest you right now?"

"Because when we were in jail and you were threatening me, I used this." I raised my wrist. "The same watch you guys gave me."

It gave me enormous pleasure to see the shock on his face. "What?"

I pressed a series of buttons on the watch. My own voice, tinny and small, rose up. *"I'll tell these cops the truth. I'll tell them the FBI planted those threatening flyers, not the MEDics. I'll tell them that you threatened me, a minor. I'll them you wanted me to set the fire at the Hummer dealership."*

And then Ponytail's answer. *"Hey, have you noticed a bunch of people around when we meet with you? Who would be more likely to lie? FBI special agents? Or a sixteen-year-old girl with an admitted history of arson?"*

I stopped the recording and looked up at him. "If you try to make me do anything else for you, or if you try to send my parents off to jail, then I will use this recording to tear the lid off what happened. It won't look so good that the FBI pressured an underage informant into risking her life."

Ponytail considered this. Suddenly, his hand lashed out and slapped the wall. The sound echoed down the corridor.

"Fine!" he finally said. "Richter and I will do it without you." He pivoted on his cane and thumped slowly down the hall.

It was over. I could go back to being me. Ellie, high school student. My parents could find another cause. Everything could go back to normal.

Only some things had changed.

I opened the door again to Coyote's room.

He was asleep, his head turned to one side, his breathing even. I thought about waking him to tell him what had happened, but instead I decided to go give my parents the news first.

Coyote and I had a lot of time ahead of us.